THE HOUSE WE BUILT

INA WILLIAMS

Copyright © 2016 Ina A Williams.

All rights reserved. No part of this book may be reproduced, stored, or transmitted by any means—whether auditory, graphic, mechanical, or electronic—without written permission of both publisher and author, except in the case of brief excerpts used in critical articles and reviews. Unauthorized reproduction of any part of this work is illegal and is punishable by law.

ISBN: 978-1-4834-5303-3 (sc)
ISBN: 978-1-4834-5302-6 (e)

Because of the dynamic nature of the Internet, any web addresses or links contained in this book may have changed since publication and may no longer be valid. The views expressed in this work are solely those of the author and do not necessarily reflect the views of the publisher, and the publisher hereby disclaims any responsibility for them.

Any people depicted in stock imagery provided by Thinkstock are models, and such images are being used for illustrative purposes only.
Certain stock imagery © Thinkstock.

Lulu Publishing Services rev. date: 10/26/2016

Dedication

For my mother, who builds me even now.

PART I

Namesakes

CHAPTER 1

Molly

First, you have to understand how difficult it is to be a black woman named Molly Grasen. In a city like Atlanta, a black woman with a name like that causes a lot of confusion—especially in a family full of men named after great black leaders. Molly's caramel skin and soft black curls only baffled people when she responded to the often asked question about a mix-raced background. She didn't have one. Both of her parents were black, her mother fair and her father dark. Both beautiful in their own way, and that is how Molly saw the world and each person in it.

Molly's mother was born in Columbus, Ohio in 1954. Columbus was no Selma, Alabama, but it was not void of a similar racial tension that existed everywhere else in the 50's. Her mother, ever the nonconformist, never let that stop her from doing exactly as she felt. So in the summer of 1962, while preparing for another year of grade school, she met her best friend Molly Hirsch, granddaughter of German immigrants. The fact that she and Molly were different didn't matter one bit. She had found something in her new friend so rare, a kindred spirit—the same fight and fire with two entirely different ways of expression. Even at seven they knew how extraordinary their connection was, so when children snickered and pointed or when teachers stared, they ignored them. This defiant love and friendship that spanned boundaries and decades was the inspiration for Molly's name. The history of their friendship made the taunting of Molly the second much easier to bear.

Molly had been born into love, strength, and audacity. Her parents were world changers. She spent her whole childhood wanting to be just like them. Her father was a community activist and youth advocate. Her older brother, Marshall, once said that their father was what people wished politicians really were. Their mother worked in nonprofit development as an exceptionally skilled fundraiser. They were the perfect match, he would find the cause and she would fund it. When Molly and her brother were very young they had moved around quite a bit, building up the world five blocks at a time. The nature of this nomadic life had lasting effects on her and her brother, even into adulthood. While the constant change in environment made Marshall an overachiever striving to be the best to earn his new friends' attention, it forced Molly out of her shell, making her a master of the art of fast friendship. She had learned to use any discomfort or awkwardness about being the new kid to her advantage. The more open she was, the more her friends were. With her mother's charm and her father's ambition, there were few hearts she couldn't win over.

When her mother found out she was pregnant with their third child, she and Molly's father both decided it was time to hang up their suitcases and put down roots. They bought a modest house in Atlanta and worked to build a new community, their family.

Perhaps because of the history of her name, or maybe because of her life as a middle child, Molly was desperate to make everyone she met feel accepted, or at least, not alone. She was sandwiched between two brothers who could not have been more different if they tried. Marshall, the oldest was a dauntless, daring, and competitive sort—always working to be leaps and bounds ahead of everyone, sometimes to his own detriment. Malcolm, on the other hand, was a quiet rebel, always slow to speak but when he did the world sat up to listen. With Molly and Malcolm affection came easy, she filled his silences with wit and fun while he offered much needed perspective when her words ran out. With Marshall, however, closeness was always an issue. As they got older things improved but there was still a certain amount of distance between them, and not just Molly, but everyone in Marshall's life. It took years for Molly to realize this was not her fault, or anyone else's. Her mother told her once, "Your brother loves you, but he needs room to grow. Your father was like that. When he's ready he'll come to you." And he did.

After his junior year in college Marshall was home for the summer and Molly had just graduated high school. Marshall asked her to go to the movies with him. Confused, Molly looked to her younger brother Malcolm for some direction. He shrugged, mouthing, "go with it," so Molly turned to her older brother and nodded in affirmation.

The ride to the movies was quiet, but that was normal. Marshall wasn't really a talker unless he was talking about changing or taking over the world. She was never fully sure which was his ultimate goal. She reached for the radio, but something told her to pull her hand back. She sat back, looked at her stoic brother, and attempted to make conversation.

"How's Adrienne?"

Adrienne was his girlfriend, they'd been dating since his freshmen year and Molly had never seen her brother's face as bright as it was when he was looking at her. Yet he'd tensed at the question. He was silent, but he wasn't ignoring her. It looked like he was steadying himself to say something.

"We broke up," he said after the long silence.

Now it was she who couldn't speak. Suddenly she felt trapped in the car. He was obviously sad about it but Molly wasn't used to seeing her brother like this, so human. All of a sudden it occurred to her that maybe her brother not only felt things, but maybe he felt them more than most. After all he didn't have a great deal of practice when it came to social interaction. Her heart began to swell at the thought of her big brother in pain. She saw his hand resting on the gear shift of his BMW, which used to belong to their father, and she gently placed her hand on his. He didn't look at her, he didn't move, he just let her hand rest there until they got to the movies. Every Friday for the rest of the summer they went out, sometimes to the movies, sometimes to dinner. They never talked much in the car, but every word her brother shared was a treasure to Molly.

She had grown to associate this quietness with an inner strength and depth that required patience to explore. She was already predisposed to optimism but her brothers taught her to hope for the best—in life and in others.

It became her mantra, her *raison d'etre optimiste*. All through college she found this resolve to find the best in others tested. By the end of her sophomore year in college she discovered there were several people who assumed her thoughtfulness was a weakness that could easily be exploited. Friends and boyfriends thought they'd just lucked out in the sucker Olympics and she was sure to medal. Even a couple of professors believed that the color of her skin somehow lowered her IQ.

But Molly had the intelligence of her father and the tenacity of her mother. What others saw as unscalable walls, Molly saw merely as hurdles, trifles she could easily mount with a little momentum. Every challenge she met gave her a quiet satisfaction and confidence that if she could just stay the course and forge ahead, there was little she couldn't accomplish.

So it was with this heart full of hope that she found herself, several years, a degree, and one great job later, in a quaint little town in Georgia. The stereotypes about Georgia being one big rural cotton field had changed greatly with a booming movie industry and all the trendy new living spaces. Molly knew there was much more to Georgia than that, and she intended to find out just how much more there was.

Her new neighborhood was about an hour outside of the city, but then so was everything in Atlanta. Molly's smile had never been as bright as when the realtor handed her the keys to her new home, a white house with black shutters and a sweet little freestanding garage that she couldn't bear to park her car in.

Buyer's remorse is pretty common among new homeowners, especially those who swoon at words like "potential" when buying a house on a budget. Molly wasn't finicky, but learned quickly that working appliances were much more of a necessity than a luxury. Alas, her boundless optimism would not fail her and Molly began to see signs of light in this house. Her faith had made her romantic that way. Between her naturally optimistic nature, her faith in Christ, and her feminine affinity for lost causes, it was possible that she would live in this dilapidated house for months before admitting one thing was wrong with it.

She was, however, beginning to dread waking up in the morning to cold showers. The rain, which was now so consistent she could set her watch by it, was seeping through the ceiling in the kitchen and the living room. She congratulated herself on her lack of furniture—*less to get water damage, glass half full* she thought to herself. As if the water works were not enough, nature decided to completely encroach by sending a family of possums to live in the garage and keep her up at night. And then there was the woodpecker whom she had lovingly named Havoc. He woke her each morning about an hour before her alarm clock. Even in this she found sweetness. Her new friends, annoying as they may be, made her feel less alone in her new foreign wood. Love them as she did, her work was beginning to suffer and with her new forty-minute commute (an hour with traffic, and there is always traffic) to and from work, sleep and warm showers were essential. So, when Havoc started his morning ritual of a hundred and eighty pecks for the third week in a row, Molly rose from her sleep, livid and determined to take back her mornings. She was sure there was a pest company that could catch Havoc and release him into a bird utopia, with lots of trees he could pound far, far away from her house.

Molly had only ever lived on someone else's property—at home with her parents, dorm rooms, then a string of apartments. The optimist in her savored the eventful milestone of calling an exterminator for her very own property and her smile was wide as a mile when Harry from Sunshine Pest Control pulled up in her driveway.

"Hi, I'm Molly."

She walked towards him with her hand extended. When she was close enough to touch him he looked up from the clipboard and took her in before lowering his eyes back down.

"Harry Mumford."

She smiled to herself. Racism in the new millennium always seemed a little too redundant to be taken seriously. She understood the dangers, you couldn't live in the South and ignore them, but she also knew the difference between an ignorant person and a hateful person. She had learned to ignore the former and avoid the latter.

Mr. Mumford was not the first man to attempt subtle insults. In fact, Molly had noticed there were several approaches, but the sentiment was always the same. Her high school French teacher, for example, a plump southern woman in her early fifties, masked her bigotry as polite concern. While others, like her astronomy professor, Mr. Warshaw, wore their malice like a badge of honor. He had never forgiven her for giving the correct answers during his pop quiz on the first day of class. He had hoped to make her look like an idiot, or worse, to let other people believe she was so he wouldn't look like one.

Truth be told, this happened a lot. People spoke to her over the phone and heard her accent, or lack thereof, learned her name, and simply assumed they were speaking to a white woman. White or black she found that the more clearly she spoke and pleasant she sounded the more uneasy it seemed to make everyone. For a while she had been very aware and sometimes self-conscious of her speech, but by the age of eighteen she stopped caring. The people who were most important to her would love her for what she had to say, not the way she said it. Everyone else didn't seem to matter that much. The best remedy for Harry's haughty eyes and lack of understanding would be grace and some good old fashioned Southern charm.

"What seems to be the problem ma'am?" *Ma'am huh? Well that's a good start.* She thought to herself.

"Well Harry, I have a family of possums keeping me up at night and a woodpecker waking me up in the morning."

Harry's eyes hadn't left the clipboard, "A woodpecker huh?"

"Yes, I named him Havoc." Harry couldn't help but smile. Signs of light.

"Hey Harry, before we get started would you like some lemonade? I just made a fresh pitcher."

He finally looked up, "I would. Thank you."

Hook, line, and sinker.

CHAPTER 2

Elijah

Elijah had been his mother's favorite prophet in the Bible. His mother was not a religious person, consequently neither was he, but the story of Elijah was one that had always stuck out to his mother during her intense and completely forced religious education as a child. It was for this reason, he was certain, that his family barely ever set foot in a church when he was growing up. For Elijah, church was about bitter goodbyes. He had attended more funerals than he cared to remember, the very first was for his grandfather who had been a pastor. He was five years old and it was the first and last time Elijah remembered seeing his mother's family. Their disappointment in her brazen ways was palpable in the stale summer air. The mood was so solemn that Elijah remembered being afraid to breathe too deeply. But it wasn't grief stretched across the pale sweaty faces of the people around him—it was pride. Of course, he wouldn't come to find that out for many years when his own ego forced its way onto his face.

Elijah had inherited his iron will from his mother. At eighteen, hers led her to break the cardinal rule of her father's house—she stood up to him. She had fallen in love and wanted to get married. Elijah's grandfather never really had any valid complaints against his daughter's boyfriend. The kid was a good boy, not in church as often as he would have liked but he had a steady job in the service and he took care of his ailing sister who was the only family he had left. However, this boy was only good enough for his baby girl until someone better came along to distract her. But Elijah's father had no intention of waiting for her to be distracted. He wanted to marry her right then. She wasn't pregnant and, although he was enlisted, he wasn't headed out to war. He simply loved her. He was all of twenty years old and felt the urgency of his feelings as only the young can. He needed to marry her. But Elijah's grandfather refused to give his blessing. He had plans for his daughter that didn't include the nomadic life of an army wife, especially now that his own wife was gone. Refusing to give his blessing was the same as soaking an ember in gasoline, so when Elijah's father tossed stones at her bedroom window, she climbed down the trellis and never looked back, until the day of the funeral.

It was almost seven years later when she stood at the front of the church to say goodbye to her father. When she turned around to find the disapproving faces of her family glaring back at her, she grabbed Elijah by the hand making her way down the aisle and outside to her battle-scarred Honda.

With her husband at war and her father buried, she drove the three hours back home to the base trying unsuccessfully to hide her tears from Elijah. He found an electric bill on the backseat, folded it into a paper airplane and handed it to her.

"Thank you baby," she said as she pressed it to her heart.

For the many dark days he had experienced in churches there were at least a few bright ones. To start, there was the wedding of his younger sister, but she made everything brighter, a fact that had won her the nickname Rae. From the moment she was born, Rae forced every dark thing away, beginning with the departure of their violent and troubled step-father. Their own father had been killed in Saudi Arabia and the loss had changed his mother deeply. Elijah was too young to remember, but there was a lightness in her that left when his father died. She was stronger, but her heart was heavier for it.

When Elijah's mother met Andy, a Gulf War vet himself, they bonded over loss. She was already pregnant with Rae when they met, so Andy waited until she was born to marry their mother.

With Elijah's father the marriage had been easy. They didn't have much, but what they had in each other was more than enough. With Andy she had found something much graver. They needed each other.

They loved each other yes, but both were grieving a life they had before loss. They were broken and trying to make sense of a life together. Still, Andy struggled to feel at home with them. There was a war inside his heart and he need somewhere fight it.

Soon after the honeymoon his depression surfaced and Andy became convinced that Elijah and Rae were driving a wedge between him and their mother.

One night after attempting to drink himself numb, he returned home with fire in his eyes and lunged at Rae, who was not quite two years old. Elijah, merely seven at the time, dodged in front of her only to be thrown into a mirror on the wall. His mother ran in from the kitchen, tears in her eyes, ice in her heart, and fire in each word. She calmly threatened Andy's life if he ever came near her or her children again, but her threats weren't necessary. Elijah saw in Andy's eyes how ashamed he was of himself. How afraid he was of what he had become. He had made their home his battlefield and his family the enemy.

In fact, that look was the last thing Elijah ever saw of Andy. Twelve stitches and two days later, Elijah and his family returned home to find all of Andy's things gone. He had left a shoe box full of money and a letter for his mother. She read it once, burned it, then sat on the side of the bed and stared at the half empty closet. It was the first of many nights that she cried herself to sleep.

From this darkness Elijah naturally assumed he was now the man of the house. He proudly helped his mother by cleaning and cooking when she worked the late shift and, when he was old enough, earning his keep working odd jobs—until the summer he met Jim Hargro.

Elijah had been at the park fixing his sister's bike while she played on the swings behind him. He didn't even notice Jim watching his handy work.

"You're pretty good at that."

"Yes sir. I've had a lot of practice."

Elijah pulled at the chain to get it back on track. He looked up to see Jim smile. He was holding a smoking pipe in one hand and resting the other on his knee. Elijah didn't know why but Jim's smile made him feel welcome, like he had known him all his life.

"Bike break down a lot, does it?"

"Yes sir, at least twice a week."

"I see."

Jim lifted the pipe to his lips and placed the thin end between his teeth. He seemed to be thinking about something. Elijah's mother did that same thing with a pencil when she was trying to figure something out.

"How old are you son?"

"Fourteen sir, I'll be fifteen next month."

"Will you now? You got a job?" Jim asked, pulling a book of matches from his pants pocket and striking one to light his pipe.

"Yes sir. I deliver papers in the morning and I bag groceries over at Thompson's market every day but Sunday."

Jim's eyes widened and he pulled the pipe from his mouth. "You do all that and go to school too?"

"Yes sir. Don't think I'm very good at it, but I go," Elijah stated honestly, no smile or shame, just openness. Jim couldn't help but laugh to himself.

"Well how'd you feel about coming to work for me?" Elijah stood the bike up and wiped the sweat from the back of his neck.

"Well sir, what would I do?" Elijah asked taking a break from the bike to give Jim his undivided attention.

"Pretty much what you're doing there." He pointed to the bike with his pipe.

"You want me to fix bicycles?"

Jim laughed out loud at Elijah's face, an innocent mixture of confusion and disappointment.

"No, I'm gonna teach you to build."

Jim had seen Elijah around town before. He was always polite, never idle, and almost always taking care of his mother or sister. Jim knew that Elijah would work hard, but that wasn't the reason he wanted to give him the job. It was something about the boy's work. He hadn't just fixed his sister's bike, he had found ways to improve it. Sure the parts were busted but Elijah had taken great care to make sure the bike, broken or not, *belonged* to his sister. The frame and handlebars had been painted bright pink, purple tassels were glued to both handles, and there had to be pieces from at least three different older bikes all to hold this one together. This wasn't just repair work, it was craftsmanship, or at least the beginning of it. This boy had potential and Jim had a hunch that it didn't end with building things.

"You mean like houses?" Elijah asked glancing over his shoulder to make sure Rae was still on the swings. She had found a new friend and was now pushing her.

"We'll work our way up to that. What say we start with the basics? You know how to fix a table?"

"Yes sir." Elijah didn't know why but his heart was beating a little bit faster than usual.

"Good. I mean, that is if you want the job."

"Oh, yes sir I do!" The confirmation had come out much louder than he intended.

"Good, I guess you'll need your mama's permission."

Elijah hated the way the statement made him feel, but he knew it was valid. He stared at the ground and gingerly nodded.

"Well bring her by the shop tomorrow and if she says yes we'll get started."

"Yes sir!"

"The shop is right around that corner there," Jim pointed up the street and made a quick motion to the left with his hand. "It's called Willie's. Just come on in and ask for Jim."

Elijah shook his head so hard it almost fell off his shoulders.

He was bursting at the seams when he told his mother about the job offer. Elijah never got riled up about anything, but he was making up for lost time with this. She could hardly say no to something that turned her man-child back into the boy she longed for him to be at only fourteen.

She and Rae were all smiles when Elijah dragged them by their hands to the shop the next day.

Elijah didn't even have to ask for Jim, he was standing at the counter finishing up with a customer when they walked in. "That's him ma! That's Mr. Jim. He offered me the job."

His mother's eyes widened and she stopped, mouth half open before she said anything. "He... offered you a job here?" She tried to point discreetly, but the action by nature is never discreet.

"Yes ma'am, that's him. Can we go talk to him now?" He started to move hastily toward the counter but was halted by his mother's hand around his arm. She pulled him back.

"Elijah, I'm not sure this is such a good idea."

"What?" His voice began to tremble with emotion, he could feel his dream slipping away. "But why not? I promise I won't fall behind in school. I'll even quit the job at the market if I have to."

She shook her head and paused. She was trying to find the right words. "Son, he's black."

Elijah did not understand. His mother spent his entire life making sure he understood that people are people, no matter what they looked like. She and Andy had friends from all over the world it seemed, so many different colors and accents that he couldn't keep track, but now all of a sudden she was refusing him his dream because Jim was black? Didn't it matter that he was a good person, that he had taken interest in Elijah, or did everything she ever taught him mean nothing to her now?

She must have seen it in his face because she gently placed her hand on his chest the way she did to calm him when he was upset.

"I'm not saying no," she said, smiling gently.

She stood and looked behind her out of the window at the group of shops across the street, then back at the counter. She said it almost to herself, "It's just that not everybody learned what I taught you and your sister."

There was something grave in her face when she said it, Elijah couldn't discern exactly what it meant at fourteen, but whatever it was, it scared him.

CHAPTER 3

An Understanding

By the summer of his sixteenth year Elijah had become widely known as the town's young carpentry prodigy. Everyone knew that if you wanted your antique furniture not only fixed, but cared for, you took it to Willie's and asked for Elijah. Jim had even begun to teach him how to design and build his own pieces. Elijah chose to focus on these things, the quality of his work and the public's general excitement, and ignore the things that made him uneasy. Things like men who seemed to think it was still ok to call Mr. Jim "boy" or the women who clutched their purses tighter when Percey, Jim's son, would approach them to ask if they needed some help. He had also learned to ignore the men wearing the confederate flag like their favorite sports paraphernalia who had begun to pull him to the side and whisper, with bourbon on their breath, that he should "go into business for himself." He didn't fully understand what all of this meant, but he was starting to.

The liquor store across the square once belonged to Frederick O'Donnell but since Frederick's death earlier that year his son Tolson had taken over. Infamous for drinking as much as he sold, Tolson stumbled into Willie's one night, mean and drunk. The culprit of his inebriation, a bottle of Southern Comfort with less than half the contents left, was swinging in one hand.

"Where's that nigger lover at?"

Elijah had heard the word before, you can't live in a small town in Georgia and not have heard it, but it was the way Tolson said it that made

Elijah shiver. The word was so full of hatred and anger, as if Jim or Percey had done something to him personally.

Tolson looked like a rabid dog and Elijah shrunk back as he approached the counter. The moment felt all too familiar, he looked at Tolson but all he could see was his stepfather. When Tolson began to swing at Elijah, he couldn't hit him back for fear that he might accidentally destroy the man Tolson instead of the demon that possessed him—the same one he assumed had possessed Andy.

Percey came in from the workshop and rushed to grab Tolson's arm. More offended than hurt, Tolson flipped the bottle of Southern Comfort and crushed it over Percey's arm. Glass, blood, and liquor flew across the counter.

"Don't you ever touch me boy, you crazy?" Tolson spat angrily.

Percey moaned in pain but his jaw was clenched in anger. Elijah could see him making a fist full of vengeance ripe for Tolson's left eye. Veins were bulging, giant tears welled in Percey's eyes, but he never hit him. Tolson must have seen his eyes too. Breathless as he was, the angry mutt in his eyes was now a cowering pup. He saw exactly what Percey could have done to him, and he wouldn't have needed a bottle of So Co to do it either. The thought seemed to rattle him and he stumbled backwards into one of the shelves. He and the shelf toppled over together.

"What's going on out here?" Jim said hurrying out from the office. "Percey!"

Percey finally looked away from Tolson and the rage in his eyes dissipated leaving a hollow expression. He looked exhausted and the color was leaving his face.

Jim grabbed a rag from under the counter and rushed to Percey's side. Two men who worked for Tolson had apparently heard or seen the commotion and they burst in the store to gather Tolson. They saw Percey's arm, Jim's worried face, and Tolson still rambling belligerently while struggling to stand; it didn't take long to figure out what happened. They gave half-hearted apologies and ushered Tolson out of the store.

Jim heard nothing, his attention was focused on Percey. There was still a large piece of glass sticking out of his wrist and Jim gingerly wrapped the cloth around the shard. Panicked, Percey reached to grab it and before Jim could stop him he had yanked the jagged chunk of glass free causing a rush of blood.

Jim shouted to Elijah, "Go get the keys off my desk!"

The truck never seemed to make it past forty-five miles an hour when Elijah made deliveries but today, as if it knew what they were up against, the truck seemed to fly. Percey was losing blood quickly and was in and out of consciousness. Jim swerved into the parking lot of the hospital while Elijah shouted for Percey to stay awake. Percey had managed to give small signs of consciousness throughout the ride, like he was trying to make his way back from a nightmare but this time, there was nothing.

The truck was barely in park before Jim threw open the door and ran inside to flag someone down. A moment later two nurses and a doctor made their way outside with a gurney, they lifted Percey out of the truck and rushed him inside. Jim was right alongside his son, holding his hand and Elijah was left behind in the truck which was still parked just in front of the entrance. He slid into the driver's seat and shifted the gear from park to drive. He looked down at his hand before he put it back on the steering wheel, it was covered in blood and shaking. He wiped it on his jeans, which weren't any cleaner than his hands, then placed it back on the wheel. Elijah steadied himself with a deep breath then carefully made his way to a parking space.

While he was in the truck he had convinced himself that he wanted to move slowly because he was being careful, but when he walked into the waiting room and saw Jim pacing, he knew that he had only been putting off the weight of reality. Everything had been so loud, and moved so fast that the last few hours felt like a blur. How could he be sure this was real? It felt too cruel to be true. Elijah hoped that if he could move slowly enough time would somehow mend all the damage that had been done and Percey would emerge from behind the emergency room doors to tell them that he was fine and that they could all go home. But Jim pacing meant no such healing had occurred and they were cursed to keep waiting in this very real uncertainty.

Jim's cell phone was in his hand, and he looked so nervous that Elijah couldn't tell if he had just hung up with someone or was working up the courage to call them.

"Where were you? I came back out and couldn't find you," Jim scolded. Elijah recognized the tone from his mother it meant "Don't you know I'm too worried to worry about you too?"

"I had to move the truck," Elijah said gently his hand raised wearily to point behind him at the door. Jim's face softened a bit as he reached out his hand and pulled Elijah into his side.

"My wife's on her way, you better call your mother," Jim held out the phone for him to take.

They made their way towards two empty chairs but before they could sit the doctor returned from behind the double doors.

She made her way over to them slowly, her scrubs still stained with Percey's blood.

"I'm sorry. We did everything we could."

Elijah had never heard a quiet this thick. The waiting room was full of people, but he couldn't hear them anymore. Jim stood frozen and Elijah waited to see what shape his grief would take.

"I want to see him," he said firmly.

The doctor opened her mouth to say something but before she could speak Jim exploded.

"I want to see my son, now!"

She pointed the way, inviting him to follow her. Elijah followed, too scared to stand still but not fully aware of the fact that he was moving. Jim pushed his way through the first set of double doors and then the second. Instinctively, Elijah stopped at the second set of doors and peeked through the round window. He could see Jim enter the room where Percey lay on the table. Jim lifted his teenager onto his lap as if he were a six-year-old boy again, and he wept. Elijah stood watching from the hallway. Even through the doors he could hear Jim wailing—he had never heard a sound like that. He felt now he was the one having the nightmare, now it was he who was swaying, hoping to wake up.

The funeral was a week later. The church was so crowded that several people left to meet the family at the cemetery or the house later that evening. Jim's wife, Eloise, cried the whole day and Elijah had never known that there were so many ways to cry. She sobbed and screamed and sat silently while rivers ran down her cheeks. When they reached the house later that day Elijah wondered how there could be anything left as she whimpered softly on his mother's shoulder.

Jim was stoic but Elijah knew that his heart still wept for his son. He had heard the wailing clearly that night at the hospital. Elijah knew that cry hadn't ceased, Jim had simply found a way to trap it inside. He watched as Jim silently drifted to the porch, then summoned the strength to join him. They stood in silence for a long time.

"I'm sorry Mr. Jim, sir," he didn't mean for the tears to start.

"For what? You did everything you could."

"No, I didn't!" he didn't mean to yell either, but he had never known this much sorrow or remorse. He was not sure how to control it. "I just stood there and let Tolson…" his voice trailed off and Jim grabbed him by his shoulders.

"Elijah, you listen to me. Tolson came in there ready for a fight and if you had tried to get in the middle we would have had two dead sons in this town instead of one."

This only made the tears flow faster and harder.

"I just don't understand why he was so angry. Percey never did anything to hurt Tolson, or anybody."

Jim was still holding his arms. "Naw, I don't suppose you would." Jim released him and turned back towards the night sky.

"Mr. Jim?" There was only permissive silence.

"I'm sorry about my mother too." Elijah didn't know why he felt compelled to confess what his mother had said on that first day, but he did.

Jim looked into the house through the window. Elijah's mother was preparing a plate for Eloise as Rae wrapped her small arms around her shoulders as far as they would reach. Jim looked back at Elijah then up at the night sky again. He was quiet for a long while and Elijah began to regret telling him. He hadn't meant to put a wedge between Mr. Jim and his mother.

"She didn't mean nothin' by it Mr. Jim, she was just scared," he assured Jim trying to backtrack.

"She wasn't scared for you son."

With six words the world changed, and understanding came like a wave in a stormy sea.

CHAPTER 4

Bixby's Bulbs

Harry had spent an hour at Molly's place, the inspection usually only took about fifteen minutes, but a little homemade lemonade goes a long way and before they knew it they were talking about Harry's son, Michael, and his love of comics. He recognized her woodpecker's name from one of his son's stories. She admitted developing a love of her own after seeing her older brother's obsession with the modern day myths.

After his glass of lemonade Harry looked the house over twice. He spotted some old mice droppings under the house. They looked old enough, but he didn't want to chance it so he set some traps just in case. For the family of possums, he put several odor deterrents in the garage. Then came the bad news.

"We don't really do the catch and release thing, Ms. Grasen. I could set a trap for him, but more than likely it would...well, I couldn't release him." Molly shrank. She couldn't send Havoc off to certain death, no matter how annoying he was. He was her first friend in this new strange place.

"Isn't there anything else you can do? I don't want him pounding my door at five am but I definitely don't want him executed." Harry laughed at the thought of a bird being executed.

"Well there's nothing else I can do, but maybe you could build him something to peck on instead."

"You mean like a bird house?" she sang, eyes beaming.

"Sure," he nodded, happy to have softened the initial blow.

Molly was inspired by Harry's idea. She began to think not only about a bird house for Havoc but a little garden they could share. And then maybe other birds would come, it would be an oasis for all kinds of birds. Maybe one day there'd be a Mrs. Havoc and a bunch of baby Havocs. The jury was still out on her own love life but who was she to stand in the way of Havoc's.

She was up all Friday night thinking about the garden, making sketches. She searched online to find a local plant nursery and discovered that her new town had no movie theater but two nurseries. She paused to question the town's priorities, and then her own. The first nursery was one of those franchises. She saw the logo and instantly the annoying theme song sprung to mind—pass. The second was a locally owned shop, it looked sweet and the owners were a cute, young married couple. One look at their adorable picture on the "about us" section of their website and Molly was ready to buy everything in stock. She quickly jotted down the address, circled it with a heart, and switched off the light.

The next morning, she rose with the kind of brightness that only a woman on a mission can have. As Molly pulled into the parking lot of the nursery she noticed that the whole shop was housed in a greenhouse, a little oasis in the center of a gravel lot. She made her way up the narrow stone path to the door and the lush green plants around her made her feel as though she were venturing into a secret garden.

When she opened the door the smell of rich soil and deep green leaves wafted out like a cloud of perfume. She didn't even know colors could have a smell. There was so much to see. The entire room was full of branches, petals, and leaves, but it didn't feel overwhelming. It felt secluded and peaceful, despite the fifteen or so customers who apparently had the same thought she had that morning.

Molly bounded up to the counter and sang a sweet morning greeting. She recognized the man at the counter as the husband from the photo of the owners. He tried to match her energy, but Saturday morning was obviously a busy time for them and he was barely keeping his head above water. He offered a quick hello and politely excused himself to help another customer who had been waiting patiently.

"I'm sorry, we're short staffed today," he confessed after returning ten minutes later. "How can I help you?"

Molly, still wearing the same smile she came in with, reached into her purse and pulled out her sketch.

"No problem. I was hoping you could help me create this." She handed the sketch to him and he stared at it for a moment smiling wider and wider, first to himself then at her.

"That depends. What is it?" She knew he hadn't mean it to, but it stung like a paper cut.

"Geez is it that bad? Well, it's supposed to be a garden."

"Ah." He said, nodding as if he saw something now that he hadn't seen a moment earlier.

"Alright, alright I can take a hint. Anyway I have an idea of how I want it set up, but I have no idea what to grow. You see, the garden is for a woodpecker." He was giving her a look, one that implied: *Are you mentally unstable or really endearing? Cause I can't really tell.*

She gave him the cliffs notes version of her beloved woodpecker's story.

He laughed, "You should really meet my wife, this is right up her alley. She's not here right now, but if you want to leave your number I'll have her call you as soon as she gets back. I'm Howard by the way, Howard Bixby." He wiped his hand on his jeans before extending it.

"Molly Grasen." She took his hand and shook it cheerfully before giving him her contact information. "Alright then Howard, talk to you soon." She folded her sketch and put it back into her purse.

"You too Molly, have a great day." He smiled to himself thinking how his wife would enjoy Molly's whimsy.

CHAPTER 5

I Thought I Knew You

In the years following Percey's death, Jim had grown older much faster. He was still kind and generous with his wisdom, but the light had gone out of his eyes. He seemed to have lost his purpose for living.

Time brought "The Lord's Vengeance" as Eloise called it. Three years after Percey died, Tolson drank himself delirious and set his shop on fire while he was still inside.

After his eighteen-month sentence for involuntary manslaughter following Percey's death, Tolson only seemed worse. He was angry all the time and even his family was having a tough time keeping him under control. A few minor incidents landed him back in jail and eventually a judge mandated that he go into rehab. Within days of his release he was back at his shop drinking himself numb to summon up his resolve. He flipped open his zippo and dropped it in a small pool of Jack Daniels he'd poured on a rug in the middle of the store. The flames were everywhere by the time two of his regulars pulled him out. His shop and several others on that block were burned down to the framework. To understand the silent smiles in the hearts of Hargro family when Tolson O'Donnell was hauled off to be committed to a local mental facility, you would have to understand that just six months after Percey's death these same neighbors whose businesses burned had sat by quietly, claiming that there must have been a misunderstanding that caused Tolson to lash out at that "poor carpenter boy." They hadn't even had the decency to use his name, Percival Lawrence Hargro.

Percey had been two months shy of going to the same college Dr. Martin Luther King Jr. attended, and in a few short years he would have been the first man in his family to receive a college degree. So when Elijah sat in the courtroom watching the judge make a decision about the fate of the man who was responsible for stealing a son from Eloise and Jim, and a friend and brother from him, he felt for the first time what he had seen in Percey's eyes that day in the store—hatred. It was that same hatred that numbed his heart the day he watched the men and women weep as flames engulfed their livelihoods. Until then, it never occurred to Elijah that God might actually exist and perhaps (now this seemed far-fetched, but) *care* about this world he had created. Broken as the world was that day in the midst of those flames, there seemed to be justice.

Seven years after Percey's death and well into the construction of the second house he and Elijah built together, Jim died of a heart attack. Everyone, including Ms. Eloise, expected that the store would be left to Elijah. After all, he had worked at Willie's for eight years. But when the lawyer read the will, all were shocked to find that Jim had left the store to his nephew, Earnest Jay. No one was more shocked than Earnest Jay himself. He had only worked in the store two summers in his life and he spent those two summers reading in the back storage closet. He was scheduled to head back to Morehouse College to finish his law degree. He didn't know the first thing about carpentry or running the shop, and he had no intention of learning.

"Look Elijah, everyone knows the shop should have been yours in the first place," Earnest Jay was whispering to Elijah in the hallway of the Hargro house after the funeral. "Why don't you stay here and run it for me? We can split the profits. I'll use my part to pay for school and when you've saved up enough you can buy me out."

Elijah was no business man, but that sounded like a square deal. He nodded and held his hand out to shake.

"Deal."

"Great! I'll have my contracts professor help me draft up the paperwork and get it to you as soon as possible."

The paperwork came a few months later with a letter.

Dear Elijah,

I know this is a lot to process, but take some time with the paperwork before signing if you need. Jeff Johnson is a lawyer in town that Uncle Jim trusted. You can take it over to him and he can explain what everything means. Call me with any questions. I'm excited to do business with you.

Sincerely,

Earnest Jay Hargro

Earnest Jay Hargro

    Elijah felt certain that he could trust Earnest, they'd known each other almost a decade, but a few months alone in the shop and one look at the paperwork, Elijah could see that he only knew half of what he needed to make the business work. He followed Earnest's advice and took the paperwork to Jeff Johnson's office.

    Jeff was away on business but his leggy brown-haired niece, Katy, was more than happy to help him. She was currently in law school and would be interning at the office for the next few months. The office was quiet with her uncle gone, so Katy volunteered to translate what she could to Elijah. She was charming and funny, an excellent teacher and an even better flirt.

    Katy was in the beginning stages of becoming one of those women who was way out of Elijah's league. She was sexy and intelligent. She may not have been a lawyer yet, but she was already a shark. She saw what she wanted and she took it. Including Elijah.

    "You know, my Uncle Jeff's clients are usually much older," Katy purred after taking down Elijah's information for her uncle. She swung around in her chair at the receptionist's desk revealing her very long, very beautiful crossed legs. Elijah grinned to himself and slowly pulled his eyes back up to hers.

"I'm not a client." He said matter-of-factly. They both knew what she was doing.

"I just had a few quick questions about the contract," Elijah finished.

She lifted her head to signify that she understood then took a business card from a small tray on the desk. She quickly wrote something on the back of the card and flipped her hair as she stood to hand the card to Elijah.

"Well I'm sure he will have excellent answers to any of your other questions," she said, holding the card out in front of her between her index and middle finger. He took the card still smiling, she was much better at this than she needed to be.

"But I hope your questions won't be too quick," she said through a winning smile before turning back to her desk. He shook his head in nervous disbelief.

Was she serious?

Elijah left the office with a pretty good understanding of the legalese outlined in the paperwork, the names of the best business schools in the area, and Katy's phone number. He laughed to himself when he spotted it on the back of her uncle's business card.

He and Katy spent the next four months falling in love the good old fashioned way—making mischief, sneaking around, and helping each other dream. But when Elijah invited Katy to Ms. Eloise's house for their weekly family dinner she refused him, for the fourth time in a row. He began to see in her the same sideways glances and purse hugging he had seen when he started to work at the store all those years ago. He spent the better part of their time together trying to ignore it, but as with most things the more you ignore it the bigger it gets.

Weekly dinners had become a great source of comfort and support for Ms. Eloise. With both Percey and Jim gone, Ms. Eloise was living in a house filled with memories and not much else. Aware of how loss could magnify loneliness, Elijah's mother had resolved to fill that house as much as possible. The dinners started as just the four of them—his mother, Ms. Eloise, Rae and Elijah, but soon the house began to fill up with family and friends. Earnest Jay frequented whenever he was on break from school along with Ms. Eloise's nieces and nephews, Jim's cousins and siblings, and before long it was like a weekly reunion. Ms. Eloise, Elijah's mother, and Rae would spend all day Saturday cooking and talking and laughing. Rae even started taking the school bus to Ms. Eloise's house after school when her mother was working late. By the time she graduated high school Rae even had her own room at Ms. Eloise's and a little herb garden on her back porch. In their grieving for the loss of family, they had built a whole new one—one even bigger and stronger than before.

On the fourth of July Elijah's mother invited everyone to her house for a barbeque. Naturally eager to please, Katy came dressed in her best and most modest summer dress. Elijah beamed with the energetic beauty on his arm and ushered her in to meet his mother and sister.

"Momma, this is Katy." Elijah said in a voice as serious as he thought the moment.

He had never introduced a girl to his family before. There had never really been anyone to introduce, any crush he had or girl he had dated had already known him and his family. That was simply a part of living in a small town. It hadn't even occurred to him to be nervous until the moment he walked into the house and saw the eager look on everyone's faces.

"Well, hello. I've heard so much about you." His mother chimed as he ushered Katy into the kitchen.

"Oh, hello ma'am, it's such a pleasure to meet you." Katy chirped, turning on all of her southern charm.

Elijah turned to introduce her to Rae who was bright and endearing as always.

"It's so good to meet you," Katy exclaimed reaching out to hug Rae.

She returned the hug sincerely, though she was taken aback, and gave Elijah a quick look to let him know she was pleasantly surprised by his new girlfriend.

"Can I help you two with anything," she asked quickly. Katy had been trained well as a southern lady.

"That's so sweet, but this is all Ms. Eloise's doing." As if on cue Ms. Eloise walked in from the next room carrying a stack of dishes and a handful of silverware.

Rae hurried off of her seat. "Ms. Eloise, I told you I would take care of all that!"

"It is not going to break my back to carry a few dishes."

While technically a senior citizen, everyone in town knew Ms. Eloise could still swing lumber with the best of them.

"That's not the point, you've already done so much." Rae grabbed the items from Ms. Eloise's arms and ushered her to the stool where she had been sitting.

Elijah wrapped his arms around Ms. Eloise and turned to Katy, who was doing her best to avoid eye contact with Eloise.

"Katy, this is Ms. Eloise who I was telling you about."

Ms. Eloise's jaw tightened and she forced a smile, she said, "You must be the famous Katy we've been hearing about."

Strained and low Katy offered a weak, "Hello." She nodded but never extended a hand.

Rae, ever the peacemaker, broke the uncomfortable silence, "Katy, just wait till you try Ms. Eloise's cobbler, it's the best in three counties."

Katy smiled faintly and turned to face Rae, "I'm sure it's delicious."

Eloise's smile fell and she glared at Katy in indignation before turning to face the dishes again.

After another deafening silence Elijah's mother tried her hand. "Rae, why don't you take Katy out back and show her your garden."

Always eager to share whatever she was growing, Rae leaped to her feet and led Katy to the back door.

Elijah stood in the corner of the kitchen frozen in anger and embarrassment.

"I'm sorry Ms. Eloise. I didn't know…I mean, I didn't mean to…"

Ms. Eloise stood and pressed her hand to Elijah's cheek and locked her eyes on his.

"There is nothing for you to apologize for."

She kissed him on the cheek and turned to leave the kitchen, before calling over her shoulder to Elijah's mother.

"Darling, do me a favor and check those pies in about five minutes."

"Yes ma'am, Ms. Eloise. I'll send Elijah out to get you when they're ready."

Elijah looked at his mother then back at the kitchen door. How could they pretend? How could they even stand to be in the same house with someone who thought so little of them?

"Aren't you going to say anything?"

Katy sat in the passenger's seat of Elijah's car glaring at him when Elijah pulled into her driveway an hour later. They left his mother's house earlier than expected and Elijah was still planning on returning to the party after he was finished, after they were finished.

"You're not even going to look at me?" Katy pouted.

"No." Elijah's voice was quiet and steady.

Katy sensed a storm was coming so she tried again, gently this time.

"Elijah I just wasn't expecting all those people to be there. I got a little freaked out."

Elijah said nothing. He kept his hands on the wheel and stared out the windshield.

"Elijah, I'm sorry but I thought I was going there to meet your family."

"You did." He said it plainly, as if her ignorance confused him. Then reached across her and opened her car door.

She sat in shock for a moment. Without looking at her he knew there were tears running down her cheeks. He knew, but the part of him that cared was still frozen in his mother's kitchen. She got out of the car, slammed the door, and watched as he sped out of her driveway.

CHAPTER 6

From the Outside In

Molly was so excited that she was waiting outside of the house for her guest to arrive. Howard Bixby had given his wife the message as promised and in the week since she had returned Molly's call about the garden, they had talked every day. The calls started as a way to get the planning started, sharing ideas and favorite flowers but, as is so often the case with people of like minds, they began to talk about the whys. This flower was her favorite because of this childhood memory, and the other favored this one because of what it symbolized. Before they knew it they were talking about people and animals and God and friendship and love. The consequence of these confessions was a brilliant plan for a simple garden and a blooming friendship between two kindred spirits.

The idea that she was one step closer to creating her garden made Molly feel one step closer to making this cottage her home. She didn't have any benches or chairs for the outside of the house yet, which made waiting outside a bit more obvious than she would have liked. If there were a rocking chair or swing she could have brought out a book and pretended to read. Of course if she had the rocking chair or the swing she wouldn't need to pretend at all. Inspired by the stream of consciousness she decided to do something instead of pretending. She grabbed her journal and an old blanket from the closet before heading back outside.

She spread the blanket on the hard dark earth and looked up at the perfect early spring sky. Soft white puffs of cotton on a crisp blue satin cloth, every Sunday afternoon should look like this. She opened up the journal and began to write about her intention for the garden and her new home.

"Hello?" a bright voice called out.

Molly looked up from her journal, shading her eyes. She had been so engrossed in her writing that she hadn't heard the car pull up in the drive. Slightly blinded by the late afternoon sun, she was able to make out the silhouette of a woman, petite but strong, with her curly blonde hair pulled into a ponytail.

"Hello there!" Molly sprang to her feet and the women wrapped their arms around each other as if they had been old friends separated for a long time.

"It's so good to finally meet you."

"You too!"

Their embrace transformed into linked arms and Molly led her guest towards the spot where the garden would be.

"Well Mrs. Bixby, can I get you anything?"

"Oh please," she tossed off the idea of a formal greeting from a friend, "call me Elsa."

As seemed to be the trend with Molly, the business was handled quickly—measurements for the garden, marks for each plot, and the plans for what would go in each one. With all of the formalities out of the way the ladies were free to dive heart first into another wonderful getting-to-know-you conversation.

"So where are you from originally?" Elsa asked now seated on the couch in Molly's living room.

The couch was incidentally the only real piece of furniture in the living room and only one of three in the whole house. The southern hostess in Molly was horrified to be entertaining in such squalor, but the only thing stronger than the pride of a southern woman was the bite of a Georgia mosquito at sunset, and they were out with a vengeance tonight.

"Well my parents moved around quite a bit when I was little but I was actually born in North Carolina."

"Really? I would have guessed you were from somewhere up north."

The irony dripped from every elongated syllable. Elsa had enough of a southern accent for the both of them.

"Yeah, well there's a little of that in there too. Two years in D.C., one in Chicago, and another in Pittsburg, but I grew up in Atlanta mostly."

"Wow, quite the seasoned traveler. So how'd you end up here?" Elsa wondered aloud. "No offense to our small town but we're not exactly metropolitan." They chuckled together.

"Yes, I've noticed. Honestly, I knew that when I bought my first house I wanted to own at least a little of the land around it, the closer you are to the city the more expensive it is so I just decided to travel off the beaten path."

"Yeah, way off," they shared a laugh again.

Elsa took a look around the room, deciding on a delicate way to ask the next question.

"So, are you thinking about renovating at all?"

Molly smiled into her glass of lemonade. She loved it when people went out of their way to be polite.

"Honestly, I wouldn't know where to start. Decorating, designing, that sort of thing has never been my strong suit," Molly admitted.

"I refuse to believe that. We just spent the past week designing one of the most gorgeous gardens I have ever seen, for a bird." They both exploded with laughter at the thought. "You mean to tell me you can't design three little rooms for yourself."

Molly thought to herself. When it was put like that it sounded really easy but the truth was that was exactly why it was so hard. She was excellent at doing things for others, it was doing for herself that had always presented the most problems.

Apparently Molly's face betrayed her every thought.

"I'm sorry, I didn't mean to give you a hard time about it. You'll do it when you're ready."

Molly was grateful for the reassurance but she recognized the truth of Elsa's first statement.

"Actually, I'd love to do it now if I had the help."

Elsa beamed, she always loved an opportunity to help.

"Well I know someone who would be perfect for the job. Let me talk to him and I'll pass along your information."

Molly's face was full of grateful surprise, "That would be great. Thank you!"

Elsa smiled in reply then stood from the couch. "I better get home. I don't want Howard to worry."

Molly walked her to the door and hugged her goodbye. She stood at the door and watched Elsa pull off into the darkness. As she watched the taillights disappear into the woods she felt the familiar pang of jealousy. She had grown accustomed to it now—anything from a couple holding hands in the market to children playing at the park brought the feeling up like bubbles to the surface of a brook. It had been miserable for a while, but she had learned to control it. It was just a feeling after all. Feelings have no bearing on what is real and, despite popular belief, they can be controlled. But one look into her empty living room and Molly knew she would have her work cut out for her wrestling those reckless feelings tonight.

CHAPTER 7

Let Me Go

Molly had loved Clint Wilkes for all the wrong reasons. Ever the artsy outsider in high school, the pretty popular guys had never taken interest in her. It didn't bother her. She had never taken to worshiping people like the other kids her age. She had intensely meaningful causes to be a part of and even if they didn't stick, they were hers for the moment. It wasn't until Clint came along during her second year of grad school that she began to understand the appeal of a charmed life. Clint was an up and coming African-American entrepreneur, even in college. With his father's money and his ivy-league education his star was on the rise.

She hated to admit it but, looking back Molly knew that part of his appeal had been that she thought he was way too cool for her. She began to make subconscious concessions. She forgave the days without a single phone call, plans canceled for impromptu meetings, one-sided conversations, and a thousand other small things that slowly became a mountain between them. She couldn't break up with him of course, he was perfect for her. He was tall, handsome, successful, ambitious, intelligent—she would have to be crazy to break up with him. Only she wasn't crazy, she was lonely, and not just sometimes but all the time.

By year three, their relationship had become less about love and more about strategy and planning. Even his proposal was an elaborate way for him to check things off of his to do list. Romantic overpriced bouquet - check, romantic music - check, expensive ring - check, moving rehearsed speech - check. She still couldn't believe she'd said yes. Her heart sank the moment she said it. How can you love someone who never seems to see you? Clint loved her, she was sure of that, and she loved him, but it wasn't marry-me love, it was stay-with-me love. It was the kind of love people cling to in order to keep from being alone. Deep down Molly knew that it wasn't strong enough to build a marriage on and she finally worked up the courage to say so two days before the rehearsal dinner. Clint had called to tell her that he was going to be a few hours late, his meeting had been pushed back so he had to take a later flight.

"How about we don't get married?" She blurted over the phone.

He was sure it was a joke, but he didn't laugh. He never laughed anymore, she couldn't remember if he ever did. In his own version of hanging on, he asked if she had thought of all that she would be giving up. Molly flashed forward to every soccer game and ballet recital that she knew he would one day miss for similar if not identical reasons and her compliant smile faded. She was resolved.

"I have." She said with certainty and relief.

The months she spent crying after the breakup were more about how little she felt, rather than how much.

It had been three years since she ended things with Clint and Molly was beginning to miss something she never had. With every year she began to wonder, with increasing intensity, what it would be like to have a man look at her and be moved by what he saw, not just impressed or attracted. She had long ago begun to crave the touch of someone who needed her as much as she needed him.

After Katy there had been a string of women, but none ever made it to his mother's house or Eloise's. Business school was the focus now and since each woman seemed eventually more disappointing than the last, Elijah began to see women as a means to a very specific end. Two years flew by—Rae finished school, the store was doing well, and things were on track for Elijah to buy it from Earnest. Then his world changed.

It was three o'clock in the morning when Ms. Eloise called. Elijah had fallen asleep studying for finals, so understandably he thought it was just a dream when she told him his mother was seriously injured.

"There's been a car accident on Miller Bridge, Elijah. You need to get to the hospital as soon as you can."

They were getting to be old friends by now, Elijah and Grief. The same long drive, the same hospital, the same dark sadness. Elijah could feel that small glimmer of hope that there was a God who heard him growing dimmer with every goodbye he uttered.

He whispered a prayer out loud to this divine stranger, "God, I'm sorry. I know it's not fair for me to ask a favor of you the very first time I talk to you, but my sister says you usually cut people slack for making mistakes like that. Please don't let my mother die. I know I can't tell you what to do, but I'm asking. Please." he bargained as he wiped a tear from his eye before it could make its way down his cheek.

Ms. Eloise, Rae, and Elijah had been sitting nervously in the waiting room for an hour before the doctor came out and told them that they had stopped the bleeding but he warned them to prepare themselves for the worst. He explained that her injuries were extremely critical, however, she was too weak for surgery.

"So what do we do now," Elijah asked urgently.

The doctor looked up at Elijah with somber eyes that he recognized all too well.

"We wait," he said softly. "For now she's awake and asking for you and your sister."

Elijah had been taller than his mother since the ninth grade. "You get that height from your father," she told him once when she found him slouching to be closer to his friends' height. He had been looking down at her for the past few years, but she never looked smaller or more frail than she did lying in that hospital bed.

"Momma?" Rae sounded five years old again and it broke Elijah's heart in a new way. Their mother looked up and when she saw them both, she smiled.

"Momma you're going to get better, ok? We're going to do everything we can to help."

Her smile fell and she shook her head, tears rolling down her cheeks.

Elijah stepped closer, "Look this may not matter much to you but I'm sure it'll thrill Rae. I had a little talk with God tonight." Both his mother's eyes and Rae's widened.

Elijah took his mother's hand, "I asked Him to help you get better."

He could feel a well of tears building up in his throat. His mother tugged weakly on his hand to pull him closer. He closed his eyes and held her. Her weak but calm voice surprised him, she hadn't spoken since they'd arrived. For a moment he was happy to hear her voice, imagining that if she could speak it meant she was stronger than the doctors believed. Then he realized what she'd said.

"Sometimes He gives us what we need instead of what we ask for."

Elijah felt his soul on fire. He stood up and looked at her. It may only have been a moment, but it felt like forever. The room was getting smaller but she seemed to be drifting further and further away, too far for him to reach her, for anyone to reach her. Tears burned their way out of his eyes as he helplessly watched her smile goodbye. Rae stood silently sobbing, without hearing a word she understood what was happening. Her mother was leaving, she was going somewhere they could not follow. The thought was too much to bear, she gently crawled into the bed beside her mother and buried her head in her neck to weep there. Elijah stood frozen watching his life change before his eyes.

Ms. Eloise entered just in time, as she always did.

"I'll stay with them," she whispered softly at his side.

Her voice was so even, so calm that Elijah wondered how she could live through all of this, again. But as he turned to leave he saw the tears on her cheeks. He left the room and made his way to the silent solitude of the stairwell. He bawled until his eyes were numb and his voice was stripped.

With his mother gone, Elijah began to remember Jim's face in the days following Percey's death. Only now did he understand how hollow grief could make you. Nothing seemed to matter—not the store, not school, even Rae seemed too far away in his sea of grief. He lay in his apartment dazed and broken for three weeks. And then there was a knock.

Ms. Eloise stood in his doorway and, without a word, she hugged him deeply. The embrace brought back the flood of tears and she let Elijah cry on her shoulder until he was finished and then she led him by the hand into his kitchen. She pulled a warm pot from an insulated bag she had brought with her and poured him a bowl of her famous pumpkin soup. When he had eaten enough, she looked him in his eyes and spoke for the first time since she had arrived.

"I wasn't really sure about you and your mother when you first started working at the store. People in this town have a way of disappointing over and over again. But when your mother came to the house that night after Percey..." her voice trailed off as she remembered her son. Elijah saw her drifting so he moved closer and placed his hand on hers. She smiled before continuing on a new thought.

"You know James told me what you said to him that night on the porch." Ms. Eloise was the only one who called Jim, James. Even the funeral program had read Jimmy Hargro.

"You should know that he always meant for the shop to be yours." Elijah looked up at her for the first time.

"James left the shop to Earnest for the same reason your mother said what she said on the first day you came to work for him. This town don't take to change fast, but just like the rest of the world it's got to learn you can either fight it and die, or take it and run with it."

She pressed her hands to Elijah's cheeks "Willie's is your place now and that's how James wanted it. Now, you got it, what you gone do with it?" She stood from the table and kissed Elijah on the forehead.

"Finish all that soup. I'll be back for the pot tomorrow."

Elijah smiled, "Guess I have to call you Ma Eloise now, huh?"

"Might as well." She winked and let herself out, closing the door behind her.

Elijah was back in the shop the next day and at the bursar's office the day after that. The hollow wasn't gone, but purpose had returned and three years later, with his bachelor's degree in hand Elijah was building more than just furniture.

CHAPTER 8

The Me You See

After Clint, Molly had subconsciously taken a break from dating. Her focus changed. There were a few guys here and there, but no one ever stood out. *A sea of grey* was all she kept thinking to herself, a haze of black and white. After a while she decided that the best thing to do would be to build up her own life. She focused on work and eventually on buying her house. Now she was focused on the renovation of the house. She had systematically made herself too busy to think about dating. She was, at least, too busy to admit the improbability of such a statement.

He was cute, not just tilt-your-head-and-sigh cute. The contractor Elsa recommended was make-you-lose-your-train-of-thought attractive. He stood about six foot three and his thick wavy brown hair with small flecks of gold made her think of ocean waves reflecting sunlight. His light brown eyes held a sadness so deep it made her want to dive in and save him. That was the first strike she noted. Men who seemed to need saving usually did and were always more trouble than they were worth. They were usually mean too. She pulled her eyes back from his strong arms in just enough time to hear the tail end of his question to her. *Something about time, time limit, time table...oh, for the renovation.*

"I'd like for everything to be done by the beginning of September."

He looked up at her in surprise or maybe it was agitation with her zealousness. Whatever the reason, his look was definitely rude. *Mean, I knew it* she boasted to herself.

"That's pretty soon for the amount of work you want done, it's almost June now."

"Too soon for the town's fastest contractor? Not according to what I've heard," she offered a healthy challenge with a big side of compliment.

Molly grew up with a father and two brothers, she knew her way around the male ego.

"Well, we'll do our best to meet your deadline." Ah the old stretch the deadline trick. She knew that one too, they had been forced to live through their fair share of renovations back in Atlanta thanks to her mother's spontaneous nature. Molly believed it was her mother's way of appeasing her nomadic spirit once she and her father put down roots.

The trick was to stay firm, "I'm not worried. I know you'll meet it." Molly declared boldly. "So when can you start?" Elijah looked up from his pad and measuring tape and met her eyes for only the second time all afternoon.

"Don't look so surprised. You had the job as soon as I found out you were Elsa's favorite person."

She could tell he wanted to smile, but didn't. *So mean!* Oh well, he wasn't there for pleasant conversation he was there to fix the house and this poor place needed all the help he could give.

CHAPTER 9

The Storm

This jerk is impossible! There is obviously something wrong with the people of this town, if he is the most highly recommended contractor here. He is rude and mean and everything out of his mouth sounds so smug. "I just need you to let me do my job ma'am." He has exactly one more time to say something smart to me before I lunge at him with his own drill.

Her father had always said Molly had a bad habit of waiting too long to say what was on her mind. She smiled through pain like a Stepford wife, but when the pain became too much she unloaded like an AK47. Bullet after bullet pierced her target until there was nothing left of her unsuspecting victims. This man...this builder, was one more "ma'am" away from his last breath.

Her mother once asked her where all of that fire lived when she needed it most. She had wondered that herself, many times. Why did it take her so long to say no to other people and yes to herself?

Take the house itself, Molly had been working as a programming consultant for youth organizations in Atlanta for the past five years. She lived in a studio apartment just outside the city that was no bigger than the living room of her current house. She could afford to live in a house three times that size, but for her it didn't matter. There was just enough space for the life she had.

"Is this how big you want your life to be forever," her mother asked over dinner one night in the tiny apartment. "You've been saving up for years now. How long are you going to wait before you pull the trigger?"

Mothers have this way of asking questions that pierce and Molly began to dream of the life she could have if she were only brave enough to go after it. She shopped for her home for almost a year before she found the cottage. Her parents were bewildered when she showed them the picture of the house she intended to purchase. They couldn't understand why she would pass up newer properties right in town for a money pit in the middle of nowhere.

"It's not about the best house, it's about the right house. And that one is mine."

Her parents shared a knowing smile realizing that they had taught her this conviction. *We only have ourselves to blame*, they reveled to themselves triumphantly.

Late spring was always fairly busy at Willie's, but it seemed that everyone had heard about the renovation work Elijah was doing at Molly's. Word had spread about the amount of work that was being done on the little cottage and the rumor was that Molly was practically going to have a new home by the time Elijah and his crew were finished. The truth was that the house needed every bit of the attention.

The cottage was built in the late 40's as little more than a fishing lodge for a wealthy man who lived in the town. In the 60's a family turned the place into a quaint summer cottage, but when their children went off to start families of their own, the husband and wife put in on the market. With the popularity of timeshares and weekend rentals in the 80's and 90's, a businessman quickly snatched it up. When the housing market crashed, rentals slowed and the property fell into disuse, becoming an eyesore. The businessman was a motivated seller by the time Molly found the property online. Despite its dilapidation, the house was solid.

"The bones are there," her father commented when he stopped by to check the place out.

The kitchen was dated and the floors in the living room were starting to buckle. Molly also hated the way the wall in the kitchen seemed to cut the living room short so she wanted to remove one of the walls to create an open floor plan. Knowing she would never ask, her parents offered to help her with the renovation if she decided to buy the house.

Even Elijah had to admit the ideas were innovative, if not ambitious, and suddenly he was getting requests from people in the town who wanted similar work done to their own homes.

Elijah was nervous, he hadn't done this much work on a house since Jim was alive. It had taken a great deal of coaxing from both his family and his staff for him to agree to take on the project. He was reluctant to take on something this big without his mentor. He worried it would feel empty without Jim.

Elijah and Jim had worked on two houses together. The first had been a major restoration, essentially a rebuild, for the town's historical society. Elijah had reveled in learning the history of the house and the old furniture that had been abandoned inside the property.

The second house they had built from the ground up. It had been a labor of love for Eloise's niece, Cara. She inherited the land from her mother, Eloise's sister, after she passed. Cara and her husband moved back to the south from California to be closer to Eloise and her brother. Eloise asked Jim to build them a home. Elijah remembered having the whole family rallied around them, like they were cheering them on. And when Jim passed those same family members helped him finish what he and Jim had started.

Now that he had agreed to take on this project he realized that his main concern should have been this woman who was clearly competing for the most bubbly employer award. She laid out muffins and coffee every morning, she even memorized who drank decaf and how people took their coffee. His crew enjoyed the attention and he was sure that most people would have found this endearing and sweet, but Elijah was annoyed. *Who is she trying to impress? Doesn't she understand that her morning chats with* my crew are only slowing things down? She is the one who set the deadline that is going to take a miracle to meet.

She also seemed incapable of making one solid decision. He asked about the cabinets and she'd made up some excuse about needing a little more time to think about the color of the tile. *What does the color of the tile have to do with cabinets,* he wanted to bellow at her. And she was always trying to make conversation, as if that were what she was paying him for. He was only a moment away from telling her this very thing when the announcer on the radio gave a warning about the storm. A severe thunderstorm was headed their way and would be in the area by nightfall. Elijah excused himself from her presence, almost politely, and gathered the crew to revisit the schedule for the day. He wanted to make sure that everyone could leave by four o'clock in order to beat the storm, but that meant working through lunch.

The goals were revised and assignments made. Confident that all was well, Molly went to the room she had deemed her office in order to get some work done. In all honesty it was somewhat unrealistic to think one would find any peace in a house that was being renovated. Unlike when she lived in the city, there wasn't a trendy coffee shop on every corner where she could escape. There was Janie's, a little diner on Third Street, but if she were really honest, Molly was never the kind of person who frequented coffee houses anyway. For her, if there was any place she felt more at peace than her home, then something was truly wrong. Present cacophony aside, that was usually the case with her new haven. There wasn't much furniture, but there was something much better in the way of comfort. Ever the optimist, she put in her earbuds, blasted her favorite melodies, and got started on some reports for work.

The music must have done its job all too well because Molly didn't even think about the time until the first flash of lightning stole her attention from the computer screen. She pulled her eyes away from the computer for the first time in what must have been a very long time because the room seemed much dimmer. Something about a dim room and silence after hearing constant noise for hours is eerie. When she went back out into the living room she was almost relieved to see that Elijah was still there packing up his tools. As annoying as he was, he was still a welcome distraction from the looming storm.

"It looks like it's going to get bad out there," she said steadying her voice after the ominous thunder.

"Yeah, I sent the guys home already. We got pretty close to the goal for the day and we can make up the time next week," Elijah said without looking up from his task.

"Alright," she said.

"We tried to push all of the unfinished projects out of your way so you should be good to go until Monday." He looked up in time to catch her jump at another loud crack of thunder. He snickered to himself but she was too shaken to notice.

"I take it this is your first Georgia summer storm," he jabbed.

"In this rickety half-built house it is," she snapped, annoyed at being patronized.

He smiled again, content with himself for annoying her, "Well, just stay away from the windows and you should be fine."

He was a little too amused for her taste. "Thanks," she mumbled as she rolled her eyes.

He grabbed the last of his tools and headed towards the door. He took one last look around the house on his way out the door and left without a goodbye. Once again Molly was alone with her very noisy, very empty house.

Despite her anxiousness, Molly was a veteran of Georgia thunderstorms but that didn't make her any less jumpy. She blamed her nerves on the condition of the house even though she knew that she had always been this way. Something about the unpredictability of a summer storm had always unnerved her. You never seem to know if the storm is coming or going, no matter how many childhood superstitions you employ.

A summer storm is restless. It's hot and full and feels like it is pacing across the sky, furious and wild, ready to explode at anyone who stands in its way. Molly figured that was why her grandmother would always make them sit still in a storm. In fact, that was how she spent many summer nights when she was a child. She could still remember sitting in the dark with her cousin, Jocelyn, and her brothers, snickering and trying unsuccessfully to keep still. She needed the memory to keep her calm at the moment. She unplugged almost every electrical appliance, grabbed a candle from her bedroom, and sat in the middle of her living room floor. Somewhere between the stillness of the room, the low rumble of the thunder, and the flicker of the candle, Molly found a warm peace that wrapped her like a blanket and lulled her to sleep.

The angry thunder woke her and she didn't know how long she had been out. She was glancing at her hand, which instinctively covered her heart to keep it from leaping out of her chest, when she realized that it hadn't just been thunder she heard. Her eyes searched the room greedily for light as they adjusted to the darkness. She heard it again, but this time it was different, sharper. She noticed the large shadow through the glass in her front door. Inside, she was her thirteen-year old self again, rocking with fear, outside, she steadied herself with a deep breath. She heard the thunder again, only it wasn't thunder, it was a knock. She almost exhaled until she realized she didn't know anyone in this town well enough for them to check on her in a storm.

She inched closer to the door and lowered her voice to make it sound calm, "Who is it?"

"Elijah, your contractor," the shadow grumbled.

She didn't mean to roll her eyes before opening the door. It was a reflex. How could one man take her, in record time, from complete fear to absolute anger? It was a superpower really, the power of a reckless villain.

"It's crazy out there," he said welcoming himself back into the house without being asked. "I had to walk a mile back down here. There's a tree down and the road is blocked." He walked to the back porch where there was a pile of equipment and supplies the crew left behind and began to dry himself with a clean rag.

"Do you need to use the phone to call someone," Molly asked, with a voice full of hope. There had to be some kind police officer or tow truck driver who could drive him home. She didn't know why, but the thought of being alone with him for any extended period of time made her uncomfortable or wary, she wasn't sure which.

"Is your phone out too or just the lights," he asked.

She hadn't even remembered that they were in the dark. Her eyes had adjusted to the darkness which seemed oddly familiar and bright now. "Oh the power isn't out. I just unplugged everything because of the storm."

A smug smile stretched out across his face as he lowered his eyes.

Is he kidding! I open my home to this soaking wet jerk of a man and this is the thanks a get? Arrogance! He's got to get out of here. She ranted to herself but all she let out was "What?" with crossed arms and narrow eyes.

He seemed amused by her defiant stance and his smile grew wider. "So, you're sitting in the dark by choice?"

"Let me get you that phone," she offered hastily to avoid her actual response. *Oh he has to go...now.*

Molly walked into the kitchen to grab the cordless phone, plugging it in before returning to the living room only to be unexpectedly struck blind by sudden brightness. She squinted to focus her eyes on the tall figure across the room. Her eyes focused in just enough time to see Elijah draw his hand back from under a lamp shade.

"What are you doing?" she exploded unable to contain herself a moment longer.

"The storm is passing, so I think it's safe to plug in at least one light," he took the phone, barely making eye contact with her.

Something about the *way* he took the phone from her hand, she couldn't say what exactly but something, set her off. The AK47 her father had warned her about was loaded and Molly squeezed the trigger, letting bullets fly.

"Are you crazy? Or do you have so few friends that you don't understand what it means to be a guest in someone's home? You storm in here, drip half of the rainwater in this county on my floors, laugh at me in my own home, make snide comments about what I do with *my* lights, and now you have the nerve to welcome yourself to my phone—no, snatch my phone—without so much as a thank you!"

In the final moments of her speech Elijah could almost see the steam coming out of her ears, but he was unfazed. "Trust me, I don't want to be here anymore than you want me here. The sooner I make this call the sooner I can get out of here."

He started to dial the number but paused. He meant for that to be the last thing he said, after all she was a client. However, there was something he simply couldn't ignore about her self-righteous tone and the way she delivered her little speech, like he was an idiot, like he'd chosen to get stuck in a storm and end up in the one place he was dying to leave every day.

He glared at her and unloaded a few bullets himself, "And what kind of lunatic sits alone in the dark?"

He dialed the last few digits of the number, pressed the phone to his ear, and glared at her before turning to face the back window.

She almost lunged at him. She was prepared for things to end badly for them both, him in a hospital and her in jail. But the storm had other plans—like a parent stepping between feuding children—there was another bolt of lightning and on the second ring of his call the power went out.

Molly discarded her father's advice to be a gracious winner and chose instead to revel in her victory as she lit the way to the fuse box in the garage. She had only made one comment after the power went out and she hadn't spoken since.

But does she have to say nothing so loudly? Elijah thought to himself. He could feel her triumphant smile even in the darkness.

They made their way to the fuse box in silence. Elijah popped the panel open while Molly stood behind him halfheartedly stretching the candle toward the panel for light.

"Do you mind?" he asked annoyed but aware he was already 0 for 2. She moved closer, but still not close enough for him to see the labels on the switches.

"Look, I can't see what's going on unless you get closer and I can't fix what I can't see," Elijah reasoned.

She knew he was right, the sooner the power was back on the sooner this handy man could go on his not-so-merry way. She stood next to him on the other side of the panel and held the candle as close as she could get it.

"Thank you," he huffed. She replied with a tight-lipped fake smile then drew her eyes to the other side of the room.

He began to flick the switches on and off but nothing seemed to be changing. Molly turned again to take a closer look at what he was doing, after a moment she found herself completely engrossed, hoping that a new switch would yield a different result. She didn't even realize that her attention had shifted until she saw him jerk away from her. Even then she wasn't sure what happened. He was grabbing his arm. Had there been a spark? She hadn't seen one. Then there was more thunder, loud and angry. Only it wasn't the thunder, it was him. He was yelling at her, but why? The candle. He was still writhing, still yelling. Why was he still yelling at her?

"I'm sorry, I..." was all she could muster. She could see it clearly now—he was the storm, restless and angry. She needed to get away from him, she had to get somewhere she could be as still and quiet as possible until the tempest was done.

"I'm sorry," she said more firmly then she left the candle on a potting table and walked back into the house.

Molly didn't want to see him again. She couldn't. But she was fairly sure he was stuck there for the night. She left towels, pillows, and a blanket for him on the couch, then retreated to the safety of her room and locked the door behind her. She wasn't afraid of him but she couldn't take any more surprises. She wanted warning before he was in her presence again. What had she done that was so awful Elijah exploded at her that way and why did she feel so chastised by him? That was what bothered her the most. In the living room, before the power went out, she actually wanted to cause him bodily harm. Now that she had, all she felt was regret.

Elijah couldn't sleep. The couch wasn't the problem, he had definitely slept in worse places than the living room of his sparring partner. It wasn't Molly either, not exactly her. It was the face she'd made when he was yelling at her, as if he'd hurt her. If he was honest, that was what he'd set out to do, to hurt her. He wanted to hurt her back for the candle, for the speech. But he knew that what he'd given was much worse than what he got. And now, even after what he'd done, here he was on her couch, wrapped in her blankets, in her house that she was paying him to fix.

Suddenly he realized what her face reminded him of—until that moment he didn't know that it reminded him of anything, but it had and the thought was torturing him. The face she made while he screamed at her, it was his face, the way his face must have looked when Tolson screamed at him—scared and confused. She was afraid of him and the thought made him nauseous. She was a pain, but she was honest. In a world where almost everything felt built on some kind of lie, she was honest and he had berated her for it. He knew then that there would be no sleep.

Molly woke with a start. She had to remind herself where she was. She felt off balance and confused. There was nothing there to startle her, the storm had been over for hours and everything in the house was quiet, except her mind. She convinced herself that a glass of water might be just the thing to calm her.

She was already in the living room when she remembered that Elijah was asleep on her couch. Too close to the kitchen to turn back now, she tried to tiptoe. The floorboards of an old house are noisy traitors and it seemed that the softer she tried to step the louder the floor squeaked. After what seemed an eternity she made it to the kitchen, but now the feat was finding the box with the glasses. *Stupid renovation,* she thought to herself. She had just gotten everything situated and unpacked in the kitchen two weeks before the crew started. Everything had a proper place, but now that the cabinets and counters were all being redone everything was back in boxes. She searched for the one marked dishes in the greedy darkness, it covered everything. She finally found the box but then there was the matter of lifting one glass without clanking the others.

Now Elijah, who had found himself banned from sleep, was awake for all of this. In an effort to avoid any further contact with the victim of his outburst, he had feigned sleep. He was doing fine until Molly seemed to have trouble maneuvering her own kitchen. This amused him and he was trying to muzzle his laughter. Every clank of the dishes, every misstep was its own punchline and after she whispered a few more self-deprecating remarks, Elijah began to wonder if it would be easier for them both if he just came clean. He inhaled deeply to calm his laughter, sat up, and lowered his voice.

"You couldn't sleep either...," he started, but somewhere between "couldn't" and "sleep" Molly, stunned to find that she was not alone with her thoughts, froze. The glass of water in her hand slipped through her fingers and crashed to the floor, shattering glass and spilling water everywhere.

Idiot he thought to himself. "I'm sorry, I didn't mean to scare you."

Her silhouette began to tremble and through the darkness he could see her moving her foot to step towards the living room.

"Don't move!" He bolted up from the couch and put on his boots.

Molly, who was both comforted and mortified, stood quietly in the darkness afraid to move or speak or do anything. She felt Elijah's hand on her back before she saw him, she flinched from the surprise of having him so close. He lifted her from the kitchen floor and walked her to the living room where he gently placed her feet on the floor. She couldn't help feeling a bit like landing after flying—safe, but disappointed.

"Thank you," she said much more softly than she'd intended.

In the dim light she caught him offer a sweet smile where the smug one used to live. She liked this one much better.

She watched as he took the broom from the back of the pantry door and began to sweep up the mess. She hadn't realized how much he knew about the house. For all his faults, he ran a tight ship when it came to his crew and they were never allowed to leave for the day unless the house was as clean as they could get it without interrupting projects in progress. He was in the house almost every day of the week and she began to understand that kind of familiarity could be deceiving. This understanding made her think of her explosion. Her explosion made her think of the power outage, which made her think of the candle. She rose from the couch and walked back down the hallway.

Elijah looked up just in time to take her exit personally and he silently punished himself for wasting an opportunity to make things right. He was almost done sweeping up the glass in the kitchen when she came back with her arms full. She set more candles and a hand towel down on the card table she was using as a coffee table in front of the couch. The towel was wet and rung in one big knot.

Seeing her come back made him feel relieved. She was giving him a chance to make things better and he wouldn't mess it up this time. He walked over and sat on the couch facing her.

"I'm sorry for scaring you earlier, in the garage" he said, not sure if there should be more or less to that apology.

"I'm sorry about burning you," she returned. He laughed, still looking at her though she wouldn't lift her face to look at him.

"How's your arm?" she asked quietly, holding her hand out to receive his.

He extended his arm toward her, "it's fine."

Molly spotted the contrary truth with her own eyes. A red welt had formed on his forearm.

"I know that trick. My dad and my brother used to try that one all the time with my mom, this is not fine." Molly quipped as she lit the remaining candles.

"Don't take this the wrong way but, have you ever thought about investing in a flashlight?"

She smiled. He was still challenging her, but this felt different. He wasn't sparring with her anymore.

"I'm sure I have like three flashlights in here, but ask me how many batteries I have."

He chuckled to himself. She lifted the rag from the table and began work on Elijah's arm. She wrung the towel out over the welt so a few drops of cold water landed on the blister. Elijah hadn't realized how warm the spot had been until the cool water landed there.

She has a brother? Elijah thought to himself as Molly laid the cloth over his arm. Somehow he had never thought of her as having a life outside of this house, almost like how children feel about their teachers, as if they only exist at school. It dawned on him that he had done that on purpose. She was a client, and Elijah had never been in the habit of making small talk with his clients.

"Thanks again for sweeping up the glass," Molly said after the silence drifted from peaceful to awkward.

"No problem. It's the least I could do after causing you to break it in the first place."

"True," Molly joked.

Elijah snickered to himself and Molly caught a glimpse of what his face must have looked like as a child. Sweet and charming, she bet he had smiled himself out of lots of trouble.

Now that they had gotten off to a peaceful start Molly felt comfortable enough to prod.

"Can I ask you something?"

"Sure," He said adjusting the rag on his arm so that the welt was covered by a cool section.

"Why are you so mean?"

She'd asked it so sincerely. Her eyes were bright and she was looking right at him.

Elijah smiled, a little surprised by her candor. "I don't think I'm mean," he stated evenly.

"Really? Well what would you call it," Molly asked too sweetly to be antagonizing.

"Focused," he said plainly. Now it was he who looked at her with sincerity.

More impressed by the answer than she expected to be, Molly kept pressing, "Ok well, why are you so focused?"

"Building things, repairing things, it's the only thing I've ever been good at. And the shop I run, the man who used to run it was the only person who ever invested enough in me to help me figure that out." He hadn't meant to be that honest.

Molly certainly appreciated it. She was starting to understand more and more by the moment. Working with such firm goals, the attention to details that even she hadn't thought of, cleaning the house before leaving it each day—he wasn't addicted to his work, he simply took pride in it. Instantly, she liked him more.

As is the case with honesty, it begets more honesty and the next few hours of darkness were filled with sincere, if not silly, conversation. Molly told Elijah about Havoc, he told her about the town (leaving off the more sordid details and sticking to the tourist charms). They talked about everything and nothing. They drank tea and ate leftovers and hinted at going to bed several times though neither pushed to follow through. They watched the sunrise from the porch and drank coffee. At about 6:30 the power came back on just in time for breakfast. He cooked while she talked and when the food was ready, she ate and he talked.

But at a quarter to eight the sleepless night got the better of them both. Elijah's yawns were closer together than his words so Molly announced it was finally time to call it a night. She watched as Elijah tried to protest with half closed eyes and smiled to herself. She stood from her comfortable spot on the carpet in front of the fireplace and leaned over the card table to collect the last of the dishes. With his last bit of energy Elijah reached out to grab Molly's wrist to stop her but his hand landed on her bare knee instead.

It hadn't occurred to Molly over the past several hours that she was wearing only a white cotton nightgown. It was easy to forget. In the darkness it hadn't mattered, neither of them could see much of anything, and by the first signs of light the conversation had made her feel relaxed and comfortable. But now, with his hand on her knee, she was very aware of her lack of attire. She was suddenly very glad she had worn a skirt yesterday, which had required her to shave her legs.

His hand was still there. Why wasn't he moving it? Not that she wanted him to move, but some sort of movement would have been better than just lying there frozen.

She was wrong, his thumb began to sweep in soft graceful circles on the inside of her knee. This was worse, much worse. She felt dizzy and delirious and extremely grateful for her smooth legs, only now she couldn't get that silly song out of her head, *I feel pretty. I feel dizzy and sunny and fine!* What a stupid thing to be thinking about at a time like this but she couldn't help it, her head was swirling. Elijah sat up on the couch. He never took his hand from her knee, her heartbeat moved from her chest down to her belly then up to her throat.

He lifted his hand from her knee and stood in front of her, placing his hand on her waist. Now she was fairly sure she wasn't breathing at all, which was strange considering that her heartbeat had moved all the way to her fingertips. She didn't mean to touch his arm but all that heart-beating and lack of breathing had taken its toll and she needed to steady herself so she didn't topple over. She wondered if the room was spinning for him too.

He must have seen the panic in her eyes, he must have liked it—that he had caused it—because he smiled. This smile was different, it was dangerous. This smile made her heart beat even faster, if that was possible, and made her miss him even though he was standing right in front of her. He gently brought his hand to her forehead and swept her bushy jet black hair behind her right ear with his forefinger. He drew himself to her and the force was like gravity, she couldn't push away even if she wanted to. But she didn't want to. She was close enough to feel his warm breath on her cheek. Then the doorbell rang.

It took them a moment to emerge from the vortex. By that the time the bell had been replaced by an insistent knock. Molly's focus had shifted from Elijah's lips to his eyes and this view was no better for reentering the earth's atmosphere. Elijah, realizing that the person at the door was not leaving, reluctantly pulled away. Too agitated and distracted to realize it wasn't his door to answer, he headed towards it. With him further away the quiet crumbled and her mind flooded with thoughts, though none were intelligible. Through the clutter in her mind she could make out a familiar voice, sweet and soft, but worried. It was Elsa.

"Where have you been?" she was saying urgently, "We've been calling you all night."

Molly was still recovering but she was aware enough to know that this seemed strange. Why was Elsa here? How was Elsa here?

Molly turned around to see Elsa walk in with Elijah.

"Elsa, what are you doing here," she managed to get out, folding her arms in front of her to cover her lack of clothing.

Elsa took in Molly's wardrobe, not judgmental, just confused. "I'm just checking on my brother."

What is it with women and their loud silences? Even though her eyes never left the road, his sister seemed to be burning a hole in the side of his head.

She was driving him back to his car which he had parked by the fallen tree the night before. The road was cleared earlier that morning and Elsa had panicked when she headed to Molly's to ask if she'd seen Elijah and spotted his car seemingly abandoned on the way.

"What?" He finally exploded.

"I'm just trying to figure out what I just walked in on back there," Elsa started calmly, pretending to focus on the road.

This would be an uncomfortable conversation to have with anyone, but there was no way that Elijah was about to have a conversation about women with his little sister.

"Nothing. I got stuck in the storm and Molly let me sleep on her couch." The car filled up with quiet again and Elijah wondered if there were places in the world that used silence as torture.

He turned to face her. "Rae, you gotta stop doing that," he pleaded.

"Doing what?" Elsa's eyes never left the road. She had always been a responsible driver. She refused to put the car in drive before everyone was fastened in their seat belts.

"Just say what you want to say," he said abruptly, hoping he was prepared for whatever it was she wanted to say.

"I don't want to say anything. I'm just curious," she stated matter-of-factly.

Elijah regretted it before he asked, "Curious about what?"

"Ok, if you were sleeping on the couch, why was Molly in the living room too? If nothing happened, why were her cheeks so red when I walked in? I'm just asking, no judgment."

Elijah knew that Elsa Rae was one of the few people who actually meant it when she said no judgment. She worried, she pondered, she even prodded on occasion, but her heart and ears were always open to anyone who needed her.

"I'm not having this conversation with you."

"Why not?" She asked, annoyed at the suggestion that they couldn't share their lives with each other.

"Because you're you, and I'm your brother." He stated firmly as if he'd said something wise and conclusive instead of short and barely coherent.

"Look I really, really don't want the details, but Molly and I are friends and I just want to make sure that she isn't getting herself into a bad situation."

"Well, that sounded a little like judgment," he muttered almost under his breath.

Was he pouting? Now she really wanted to know what happened.

"You know what I mean," she said refusing to indulge his insecurities.

"No," he lied. He knew exactly what she meant. Since Katy, Elijah's romantic life had consisted of a series of one-nights strung together with loneliness and desperation. There was, ironically, no love involved in his love life.

"Elijah, I'm not judging you I just know you. You have a great heart, you just don't want anybody else to know."

"Look, your friend is safe. Nothing happened, we just talked." Spotting his car on the opposite side of the road Elsa made a quick U-turn and parked her car behind his. She turned to face him and took one long hard look at him.

"Talk," she demanded.

Elijah told her everything, the fight, the blackout, the blowup, and the conversation. When he got to the last part his eyes were soft and he could not seem to stop smiling. Elsa Rae began to see in her big brother something she had not seen in almost a decade, hope. He was bright with it and the light was contagious. She began to smile for him. He even shared the almost-kiss, though he left out the specifics of the buildup.

Then, in true Elijah fashion he attempted to undo everything with, "See, nothing."

Elsa shook her head. "Elijah, tell me you understand that more happened to you last night than in the last ten years of you sleeping around with all of those girls."

"Rae!" It was an accurate picture, but the fact that Elsa Rae was the one painting it made it sickening to hear.

"You like her." She said it so plainly. Like it was obvious, like anyone in the world could see it, if they were looking.

He couldn't even bring himself to refute it, but he definitely wasn't going to admit it to her either.

"Thanks for the ride," he said turning to exit the car.

PART II

Who We Are

CHAPTER 10

Closed Window, Open Door

"Did you ask her yet?" Elsa Rae blurted before she was all the way in the door of the shop. Elijah was still with a customer which made ignoring her question much easier. She politely greeted the patron then patiently waited until they were alone in the office before reviving the subject.

"Well?"

"Well what," he answered busying himself with receipts instead of looking up at her.

"Did you ask her out yet?"

"Who?"

Elsa Rae said nothing, silently daring him to keep up the facade.

"Ask who out," he said again, trying desperately not to blow his cover.

"Fine, be that way," she said flatly as she turned to leave. "But the window is closing Elijah, and I'd hate to think of you going through the rest of your life with only me knowing the truth about how you feel."

It was quite an exit line and she had timed it perfectly. The door closed just as she finished so that her words hung in the air like children mimicking echoes—way too loud and annoying.

She was right of course. He could feel his window narrowing by the day. His interaction with Molly had lessened significantly. Their conversations were brief and straightforward. She seemed to have a much better handle on what she wanted to see in the house and most days she was gone before he arrived and still out when the crew left for the day. He was beginning to miss her indecisive and long-winded chatter, her chipper greetings, and her annoying ability to make everything funny. The worst part of it all was that if they kept this pace up he and his crew would actually finish by the impossible deadline she set. This would not only mean she was right, but that the chance to see her at all would be over. That seemed to bother him most, not seeing her.

It was her fault. Molly was convinced she had wanted Elijah to ask her out too much and that was why he hadn't. So what if they had an amazing conversation and a heart-melting moment. *Stuff like that happens all the time, right?* She wasn't sure that it actually happened all the time, but she was fairly sure it was possible for people who hadn't forsaken their love life to focus on that of a woodpecker. She didn't want to blow the situation out of proportion. She would be professional and conduct herself with decorum. As a matter of fact, she would even go a step further and take constructive criticism. Elijah made a comment about her inability to make decisions. If she was slowing down the process that could easily be rectified, even if that meant staying up till one in the morning video chatting with her mother in order to pick a tile for the kitchen.

There was no reason to make herself uncomfortable by being constantly present. She didn't always have to be at the house while they worked. She believed Elijah and his crew were trustworthy men. Molly decided to make herself scarce. She had plenty to do at work and several places to explore in her new town.

The house was coming along beautifully and at this rate the renovations would be done before she knew it. Molly wasn't sure why, but the last fact made her both relieved and sad.

Strange how denial sneaks up on you—you never knew you were lying until the truth accosts you in the hallway of your partially renovated home. Elijah was packing up preparing to head out for the night when a weary Molly returned home after a grueling commute from work. She poured herself onto her couch, certain she was alone. When she found that she was not, she wasn't startled—not the way she was in the kitchen the night of the storm, more like someone realizing they're not alone after belting a song in their underwear.

"Hi," Elijah said softly.

"I'm sorry, I thought everyone was gone for the night." Molly replied as she quickly stood from the couch.

"No need to apologize, it's your house. I was just headed out." Elijah said attempting to reassure her.

"No, I know it's my house I just meant sorry if I scared you," she resisted the urge to be annoyed.

"You didn't," he said opening the front door.

"Why didn't you ask me out," she asked. The loudest silence of all time followed her question. It was full of self-doubt and actual southern crickets who seemed ready to the task of orchestrating this awkward moment. Elijah set down his tools on the porch then slowly made his way back inside.

"I mean I'm sure I'm not supposed to ask that. I should take a hint and all that, but I just figured I'd ask...since I really, really want to know," Molly stated plainly.

After another moment of silence her mouth opened slightly and she shook her head, "You know what, never mind. This was weird enough already. I shouldn't have said anything. Just forget I brought it up."

Elijah sank onto the arm of the couch and considered carefully before responding. "I can't do that," he finally sighed.

"Can't forget about me bringing it up or can't ask me out?"

"Either, both," he said with his gaze fixed firmly but softly on her.

"Because I'm your boss?" She teased him.

"I prefer to think of you as my client."

"Of course you do," she said smiling.

His face softened, "It just wouldn't be smart."

"But you want to?" Her chin was lowered, her eyes softly locked on his.

This was a trap he understood, but one he felt inclined to enter.

"Want to?" he asked, feigning confusion.

She smiled and lifted her chin now, holding his gaze. "Ask me out."

The corners of his mouth curled into a mischievous smile and she grinned in reply.

"Ok then," she relented, then made her way to the front door and held the screen open.

"What, you're kicking me out?"

"No, I'm letting you leave."

His brow furrowed as he tried to read her mood.

"Look, Elijah, I get it. I know how much your work means to you. I'm not going to complicate either of our lives by trying to mess with that. You're off the hook." Molly explained.

More disappointed than relieved, Elijah peeled himself from the arm of the couch and gently brushed past Molly through the narrow frame of the door. He reached down to pick up his tool box as Molly pulled the door closed.

"Besides," she started from behind the screen door, "that impossible deadline seems less impossible by the day doesn't it?"

There it is, he thought to himself. He knew that was too easy. Elijah turned to offer a defiant smile over his shoulder but the scene caught him off guard. Molly stood in the doorway, her shoulder resting on one side of the frame and her legs crossed gracefully to the other. Her arms were folded in front of her and, with the light from the living room glowing softly behind her, she engraved herself on his memory.

CHAPTER 11

Breaking Ground

"Who you trying to sound good for," Earnest Jay mocked when Elijah answered his phone an octave lower than his normal voice. Elijah hadn't realized he'd done it until the Atlanta area code on his phone screen resulted in a man's voice rather than a woman's. Secretly, perhaps even secret to himself, he was hoping it was Molly.

"Earnest?"

"Yeah, it's been forever. How are you man?" Earnest asked brightly, but Elijah noticed something about his voice sounded different. Not wrong exactly, but strange.

"I'm good man, the shop's doing well. Business is really picking up."

"I'm not worried about that, how are Rae and that botanist?"

Elijah laughed out loud. When Earnest and Elijah first met Howard Bixby he was always only "that botanist". Elijah, ever the over-protective brother, had always been pretty hard on the few guys who came to call on his baby sister. Earnest Jay was his partner in interrogation. When Howard got the official seal of approval Earnest and Elijah took to calling him Bix for short instead.

"They're fine, grossing everybody out as usual. How are you? Everything alright?"

"Yeah, yeah it's fine," Earnest Jay answered, almost convincingly. "I'm thinking about heading home in a few weeks."

"Oh cool man! We gotta hit up Grace's while you're here."

"Man, I haven't had sweet potatoes like Ms. Grace's since I've been in Atlanta."

"I'm sure you haven't."

"You can bring whoever you thought I was when you answered the phone so I can meet her," Earnest joked.

"Who says I thought you were anybody?"

"Elijah please, that's your Tara Fredrick voice. You've had it since the tenth grade. I know what I heard."

Talking to Earnest Jay made Elijah realize how long it had been since he had a true friend. There was Elsa, but closeness with a sister wasn't the same. Elijah understood that there were parts of his life that he could only share with someone who truly knew him and loved him anyway. Rae would, for better or worse, always see her big brother. But with Earnest Jay all he had to be was himself. He missed having a friend like Earnest, and maybe more than that, he had specifically missed his friend Earnest. It was this tether he felt being pulled more and more in their conversation as Earnest's voice would sink and drift off, as if happiness were some memory he was trying to recall. But when he denied for the second time that anything was wrong Elijah resolved that whatever the weight was, Earnest wasn't ready to share it just yet.

With Earnest's visit on the horizon Elijah got it into his head to buy the shop once and for all when Earnest arrived. He knew Earnest was dealing with something and figured that taking the shop off his hands would be one less thing on his plate. He convinced himself that was his motive. The real reason, while equally noble, was far less selfless.

Outside of his old GMC truck, which he'd restored with Bix, Elijah hadn't owned much more than the clothes on his back. He didn't even own the small place he lived in—a carriage apartment in the back of Widow Liddell's place. She let him have it for obscenely low rent after he fixed the armoire in her room. It had been a wedding present from her late husband. She was so moved by his restoration of it that she had trouble charging him anything at all for rent. But Elijah could hear his mother's voice, and living for free in someone else's home would never have sat well with her. He insisted on paying something, so she named a small fee and to make up the difference he acted as her resident handyman. She never asked, but he always offered.

Elijah liked his life the way it was. He never felt he needed a lot because he always felt he had enough. But owning the shop was different. It was a sacred rite of passage that Elijah was anxious to begin.

It was that excitement that made him worry when two weeks passed without word from Earnest Jay.

"Jay, it's Elijah. Just checking in to see when you're headed this way. Call me."

Elijah had enough to deal with but on top of everything else there was Molly, or rather the looming end of the renovation, that was causing strife. The deadline Molly had set was quickly approaching and Elijah began to doubt he would be ready, even if the house was.

Molly was onsite during the work more now, but not nearly as much as she had been in the beginning. The more he saw her, the more he wanted to see her and the more time she spent away, the harder it was for him to pretend he didn't care. She was cordial and kind and professional, and it was driving him crazy. Why couldn't she just be a regular woman and yell at him for blowing her off? At least then he could go back to being annoyed with her. But the more he talked to her, the more he watched her talk and laugh with the crew, the more he realized how truly un-annoying she was. The frustrating part was that the more he thought about her the harder he worked in order to stop thinking about her, and the harder he worked the closer they got to finishing.

***

"I can't believe we met that crazy deadline," Drew, one of the crew members, mused as he finished the last swig of his beer. The crew was gathered on the front porch for some well-deserved downtime after their last day.

"I never doubted you," Molly beamed as she made her way back outside with two more beers in each hand for the men who were running low.

Why does she have to be so damn beautiful? Elijah thought to himself. She was wearing a turtleneck sweater and a pair of jeans. There was nothing truly glamorous about either, but both the jeans and the sweater seemed to highlight all the best features of her figure.

"I'm kind of sad though," Molly admitted, after handing the last bottle to Elijah without looking at him. She wasn't ignoring him, she was just playing hostess. It didn't matter, he still hated it.

"You're going to miss having eight sweaty guys destroying your house and waking you up in the morning?" another crew member chimed.

"Well, I mean I won't really miss any of *that*, but..." Molly smiled as she reached to take back her own glass of wine which she had handed to Drew before going into the house. She raised the glass to her mouth and Elijah watched as her lips closed around the brim of the glass.

"What else was there?" one of the crew members joked and they all broke into laughter. The laughter jarred Elijah from his trance. He shook his head as if to nod off sleep.

The laughter of the crew fell away like fall leaves, slowly and in no particular pattern. They savored the quiet for a moment taking in the night sounds. Elijah looked up at Molly who was resting her head against the railing with her eyes closed. He studied her, trying to imagine what she was thinking.

"This," she said with her eyes still closed. "I will definitely miss hanging out with you guys." She opened her eyes to find Elijah smiling at her. Her cheeks flushed before she lowered her eyes timidly.

Elijah lingered when the last of the crew members left. After helping her cleanup on the porch he took his precious time collecting the last of his tools and loading them onto his truck. On his very last trip he realized there were no more ways to stall. All that was left to do was say goodbye, but he wasn't ready for that.

"That's the last of it," he said from the frame of the door to Molly who was standing in the kitchen washing the few dishes in the sink. She jumped at the sound of his voice, but was trying to play it cool now that she was facing him. He was really going to miss how cute she was.

"Oh, okay," she said brightly. "Well thanks again for everything. You guys really did a great job." She wiped her hands on a dish towel that had been lying on the counter beside the sink.

"Our pleasure," Elijah offered. He sounded like he was pretending to be someone else. Someone less nervous.

They stood in the silence for a moment, both hoping for something to say but there was nothing.

"Okay, well I guess I'll see you around," he said making his way out of the door finally.

"See you," she lifted her hand to wave but he was already outside.

Elijah tossed his tool box into the bed of his truck in frustration. What was his problem? Why couldn't he just say something? Anything? All he could hear was Elsa Rae's voice giving him that speech about a closed window. He was on his way to the front of his truck when he heard Molly's voice again from the porch.

"Hey, you forgot something," she ran down the stairs with a level in her hand.

"Here," she held it out and he took it from her slowly, looking only at the level and not at her.

"Thanks," he said quietly, unsure of what to do or say next.

"Sure." She turned to reenter the house then changed her mind.

"I meant what I said before."

"About what?" Elijah asked, his eyes now firmly locked on her face. He was secretly hoping she was brave enough to say what he could not.

"About you being off the hook," she made her way towards him, she was frustrated, but she wasn't picking a fight. "You don't have to…"

She never finished the sentence. Elijah's lips were on hers and she could hear him breathing her in like the first breath of air after a long swim. Her eyes closed slowly. *This feels like swimming,* she thought to herself, *or drowning,* and the thought roused her. She pulled away. They stood apart but her eyes remained closed.

"Okay," she sighed.

"Okay?" Elijah growled. Without looking at him she could feel the old Elijah creeping back in, with his walls and fences.

"What does that mean," he grumbled.

"That was actually what I was going to ask you," she took another step back and opened her eyes.

This is worry, she's worried, Elijah thought to himself. He was equal parts relieved and taken by her.

"It means I'm cashing in my rain check for our date."

He wasn't sure why he was so nervous. Elijah had been out with an impressive number of women. Granted it had been a while, but it was just like riding a bike right? Not much had changed in the year he'd taken a break. Although, if that were true then why were his palms sweating? Why were Stevie Wonder lyrics swirling around in his head? And why couldn't he find one shirt in his whole closet that didn't make him look like he hadn't been on a date in a year? He took a deep breath and steadied himself as he made his way onto Molly's porch.

Elijah could barely catch his breath when Molly opened the door. She was wearing a red dress that hugged her the way he wanted to at the top and flared out at the bottom. A delicate gold chain rested on her chest and diamond studs donned each ear. It was simple and perfect. He must have been silent for too long because she looked down at her dress then back up at him.

"What," she asked, not quite nervous but definitely curious.

"You look beautiful," he said without hesitation.

Her cheeks flushed and she smiled, lowering her eyes. "This old thing," she teased.

Elijah began to understand that for all the beauty she saw in the world around her, Molly may never have noticed how much was her own reflection.

"I wasn't talking about the dress," he said with his eyes fixed on her. He refused to look away until she met his gaze. She did.

"Thank you," she whispered, eyes wide with innocence. "You clean up pretty nice yourself," she returned.

Elijah felt warmth rise in his own face, but quickly changed the subject before any color appeared. He drew a bouquet from behind his back then ascended the stairs to hand them to her.

"Thank you," she chirped and her hand brushed his as she lifted them. She motioned for him to follow her inside.

"These are so beautiful," she doted as he sat at the kitchen table and watched while she placed the flowers in a vase.

"You're kind of an old school romantic aren't you?" It was more of a statement than a question and she glanced up at him to see him smile coyly.

"I see you're not any better at taking compliments than I am," she laughed.

"Ok, just one more sec," she said walking toward the couch and picking up a small black sweater that was laying across the back. She put it on quickly and turned to face him. "Ready," she declared as he rose to open the door for her.

Lilly's was a little restaurant on a lake. It was charming and quaint and Molly had never been there. It was the romantic go-to restaurant in her new town and it had all the makings of Molly's new favorite spot with one exception, Elijah seemed to have several admirers among the staff. The hostess greeted Elijah a little too warmly for Molly's taste and the waitress was being entirely too attentive to him once they were seated. Molly bared all of this, in her own opinion, with a great deal of grace but when the waitress agreed to bring "sweetie" back another beer after completely ignoring her almost empty glass of wine she began to suspect that quiet, mild-mannered Elijah had a well-deserved reputation in this small town.

"Why do I feel like I'm about to get an influx of hate mail," Molly joked.

Elijah choked out a laugh, "Wow!"

"You don't think that's a fair observation? The women in here are burning holes in my head with their eyes. What did you do?" Molly asked with an urgent whisper.

"What did I do?" Elijah avoided the question. "Who says I did anything?"

Molly put down her fork and sat back in her chair waiting for a better answer.

Both convicted and enchanted, Elijah relented and shared the mild version of his dating history.

"Oh my gosh. You're that guy," Molly sang pretending to be judgmental.

"Was. I *was* that guy," Elijah corrected.

"Nice save." Molly said, not at all convinced as she picked up her fork and returned to her salmon.

After dessert they enjoyed two dances on the back porch of the restaurant where the jazz trio was playing a few classics. An enchanted Molly thought the night couldn't be more perfect, then Elijah suggested a walk along the lake.

After a few minutes of casual conversation and laughter, Molly asked the question that had been on her mind since dinner, "So who's the girl?"

"What girl?" Elijah asked, assuming she was talking about one of his admirers from inside the restaurant.

"The girl who inspired your reckless and wild dating season. There was a girl, right?" Molly asked a bit relaxed from the drinks and dancing.

The brisk breeze from the lake swirled around them. Elijah wrapped his jacket around Molly's shoulders. It was too big for her and she looked like a girl wearing a football player's letterman jacket. All of a sudden Elijah really wanted to be a football player.

"You don't really do small talk do you?" He smiled.

"Come on, spill," she goaded.

"What is this, a slumber party? She was nobody, just a girl."

"Aha! So I was right! There's always a girl," she continued now a few steps ahead of him.

"Was she mean?" Molly asked over her shoulder. There was something so sweet about the way she asked it, like she was asking if he was okay.

Elijah couldn't help smiling before he answered, "Not to me. But to someone I cared about."

Molly looked at him for a long time before turning around again. She began walking in silence for a few moments before asking, "Why don't you let people see you like this more?"

The question struck Elijah, and rather intensely. This was the kind of question that Elsa would ask him. In fact, it was a question she had asked him several times before.

"Like what," he asked dodging the question.

"I don't know, protective and, not exactly kind, but noble maybe."

Molly turned to find Elijah only an inch from her face. She breathed in slowly attempting to catch her breath, but what she caught was his scent—wood, freshly washed clothes, and beer. Separately these things seemed too mundane to cause excitement but together they were intoxicating. The spell was interrupted by a shuffle in the grass.

"What was that," Molly worried as she looked in the direction of the sound, but there was only darkness.

"What was what?" Elijah asked.

This time the sound was louder and Elijah heard it too. Molly's grip on Elijah's arm tightened and he smiled as her eyes searched in the darkness for something to run from. Then the culprit emerged victoriously. A frog leapt from the tall grass towards Molly and she jumped into Elijah's arms. Almost useless with laughter, Elijah obliged her girlish tantrum by heading to the car but not before pretending to throw her in the grass.

"I had fun tonight," Molly said as she ascended the stairs and sat on the porch railing.

"Me too," Elijah seconded as he followed her up the stairs. "What are you doing tomorrow?"

Molly smiled before leaning into one of the posts on the porch towards him. "I don't know. What am I doing tomorrow?"

"Horseback riding," he stated confidently.

"I am?" Molly asked, her eyebrows furrowed in doubt.

He laughed. "Yeah, my buddy Carl has a stable a few miles from here and he's great with beginners," he reassured her.

"Really? Well what comes before a beginner? I think I'm that," he laughed again and Molly soaked it up.

"I like you like this," she said.

"Me too," he said, and he leaned in slowly, smiled a warning then pressed his lips to hers softly. He made his way around the post and kissed her again, stronger this time. He placed his hands on either side of her neck as he cradled the back of her head with his fingers. Molly's hands floated slowly up his back and she drew him closer to her. His hands moved from her neck to her back and he lifted her to her feet. She stood, clumsily bringing her hands to his chest, first for balance and then to push him away, gently. She lowered her head.

"Sorry," he whispered.

"Don't be," she said plainly, "it's just...I just..."

"Need to go slow. I understand," he said raising his hands in compliance and taking a few steps backward.

She took a step back too and answered more to herself than to him. "Yeah, something like that."

"No, it's fine. Slow is good," Elijah convinced himself before holding out his hand for her to shake.

"I'll see you tomorrow."

Molly laughed then took his hand. "See you tomorrow."

The next morning Elijah went to the shop for a few hours to get some things done before picking Molly up. He was headed out of the door, yelling out the last of the tasks for Drew to finish, when he backed into Earnest Jay as he entered the store.

"You treat all your customers like this?" Earnest Jay teased.

Elijah opened his mouth to apologize before realizing who he was. They embraced each other without a moment's pause.

"It's good to see you man," Elijah said before releasing his friend.

"You too," Earnest responded, but Elijah could hear the weight in his voice again.

"When did you get in?" Elijah asked pulling him to the side to let another customer in.

"Just now, I haven't even stopped at the house yet." He said pointing to his car parked outside.

"Missed me that much, huh?" Elijah joked.

Earnest let out a short laugh. "You headed out?"

"Yeah, I've got some things to take care of." Elijah, said a little too professionally.

Earnest's eyes narrowed. "I see. With the new Tara Fredrick, I presume."

Elijah shook his head in disbelief, same old Earnest.

"Well, look can we meet at Grace's later?" Earnest's question came out more gravely than he'd meant. Elijah could see it had something to do with what had been bothering him.

"Yeah, is everything cool?"

"No worries, we'll talk later, you go on your little date," Earnest evaded.

Elijah was concerned but knew he would have time later to get to the bottom of his friend's new melancholy.

"It's just a horse," Elijah teased Molly as she stood in front of the intimidating steed and extended a shaky hand to rub its nose. Carl and Elijah had been waiting patiently for her to complete this first small feat before mounting the horse.

"A very large, really strong, and infamously temperamental animal," Molly whispered urgently.

"Seriously, just pet the horse already," his patience fading.

"How do you know it's just me? Maybe he isn't any more ready to be rubbed than I am to rub him," Elijah shook his head, gently placed his hand on hers and moved it to the bridge of the horse's nose. Molly let out a whimper but after a moment her hand relaxed and she began to move it with ease and comfort. The horse must have felt the change as well because he rested his nose under her arm as she rubbed it.

"See," Elijah said now moving to rub the horse's neck. "What do you think? You ready to ride yet?"

"Do I have a choice?" she asked peering at him from around the front of the horse.

"No," he stated matter-of-factly.

He made his way toward her and placed his hands on her waist to help her up onto the horse. Under normal circumstances his touch would have thrilled her, but she was much too concerned with not spooking the horse to think about anything else. Elijah on the other hand, having considerably more practice with livestock was comfortable enough to note not only the shape of her waist, but also the scent of her hair, sweet and flowery, like she'd just washed it.

Once she was on the horse Molly needed to move forward so Elijah could get on behind her but she was afraid to move too quickly so she inched forward slowly, whispering "Good boy" with each small scoot. Elijah laughed and when she was far enough forward he mounted the horse behind her. He was close enough to feel that she was holding her breath. He couldn't contain his laughter.

"What is so funny?" she asked tensely.

"Horses don't get spooked by breathing. You can exhale."

"You're enjoying this aren't you," she said turning a bit before tensing up again.

"I really am. And 'good girl' would be more appropriate if you're trying to calm her."

"This horse is a girl?" The horse brayed as if in response. "No wonder she didn't want me to touch her, I'd be mad if someone thought I was a boy too!"

Elijah couldn't help laughing out loud. Molly could feel his belly moving behind her and it made her feel calmer.

"What's her name?" she asked sweetly.

"Bertie," he answered.

She smiled to herself and took a deep breath as Elijah quickly snapped the reins and the horse started a slow but steady trot.

"So, horseback riding," Molly started after a few minutes of quiet. Bertie had slowed to a rather steady walk now and Molly was taking in the view.

"Yeah, my mom and my step father used to bring me out here on my birthday. We couldn't really afford lessons or anything, but my mom knew I liked it so..." Elijah let his voice trail off as he reached around her to tighten his grip on the reigns. What he was really after was a tighter grip on Molly.

"I haven't really heard you talk about your mom much, are you two close?" she asked.

"We were. She passed a few years back," he said quietly.

He hadn't talked about his mother in a while, he hadn't needed to. It felt strange to be talking about her now and he suddenly felt very uncomfortable.

Molly turned as far as she could to look at him "I'm very sorry to hear that. I know that must have been hard."

That was it. No, sad story of her own to level the playing field, no prying into the inner workings of his heart and mind, just sincere condolences. He appreciated that.

They rode in silence for a bit. Taking in the lush fall colors around them and enjoying the crisp autumn day. The sky was one big cloud, but the day was bright and the gray sky seemed the perfect backdrop for the towering trees.

"It's so beautiful out here," Molly almost sung the words she was so enthusiastic. The sentiment was for herself, but she didn't mind if Elijah overheard.

"I'm not quite sure how you do that," Elijah said smiling.

"Do what?"

"Look at everything like it's brand new. I mean you did it all the time with the house and now out here."

"Is that why you were always so annoyed with me?"

Elijah felt a little embarrassed to admit it now, but that was definitely what annoyed him most about her when they first met. She was like a child, always so deeply impressed by everything and everyone. He wondered if it was as exhausting to live as it was to watch.

"Well if you think about it, it is all new," she started bravely. "I mean you may have seen this view before, or ridden this horse, but you've never done it with me." She said leaning her head back and resting it on his shoulder.

Elijah paused to think about what that meant. That even though he'd been on this path many times before, it was brand new today, because Molly was with him.

"And you've probably had new experiences since the last time you were here, met new people, and all those things help change your perspective. The view may not be different, but you are." She finished.

Elijah was suddenly intimidated. With one sentence, she had made sense of life.

"So what brings you home," Elijah asked Earnest after they placed their order at Grace's. Elijah had noticed that Earnest wasn't sporting his usual clean cut shave and haircut or a snazzy lawyer suit. Earnest had always dressed up, long before he passed the bar, even before he left for college. Everyone figured that he decided to be a lawyer at age twelve because he already dressed like one.

"Just needed to get away." Earnest buried his head in the drink menu just as the waiter made his way to the table with their entrees.

"They stressing you out over there?" Elijah lifted his elbows from the table so the waiter could put his food down.

"Man," Earnest huffed, sounding too exhausted to elaborate. They paused to bless the food, then both men dove head first into their meals.

After a few moments of eating in silence, Earnest remarked, "I think I'm going to stick around for a while."

"Really," Elijah looked up from his plate. He was happy to have Earnest home, but the thought that he was planning to set down roots in town made Elijah nervous.

"Yeah, Atlanta's getting to be too much. I was thinking I'd come help you out in the shop for a bit," Earnest said between bites.

Elijah paused, almost choking on his food.

CHAPTER 12

Everything

The thing Elijah loved most about spending time with Molly was that he didn't have to say much. She didn't over talk but she knew how to fill the silences. She understood when to talk and when to listen. He had come to realize that she wasn't nearly as afraid of quiet moments as he'd originally assumed she was. In fact, in the weeks following their first date they had grown quite comfortable with their little silences. She would read a book on one side of the couch while he read the paper on the other. Or she sat and rested in the living room while he did the dishes. Every once in a while one would look over at the other and they'd smile before returning to whatever it was they were doing.

One night though, the sweetness of the quiet was impeded by a sort of lingering need to speak. The silence became an annoying buzz in an otherwise peaceful room. She set down her book and approached Elijah sweetly.

"Hey," she started and brushed her hand along his forearm. Unable to resist such a sweet and open gesture he turned to her. When she asked him what was wrong, her eyes were full of so much sincerity that he could hardly refuse to tell her.

He confessed that he was worried about Earnest Jay. Since he'd gotten back to town he was quiet and withdrawn. Elijah couldn't seem to reach him and he didn't know how or where to start. His work in the shop was improving, which only worried Elijah more, Earnest had never liked working there. Elijah was afraid that whatever was bothering him was also changing him.

"And you're sure it's a bad change?" Elijah looked up at her confused. He hadn't really thought about it, but he didn't see how change could be good.

"I mean, for you working in the shop was about growing up and healing, right?"

Elijah nodded in affirmation, he had not realized how much she really listened to him.

"Then maybe that's what Earnest Jay needs now too."

She was sitting close to him with her hand in his. He pressed his other hand to the side of her face and kissed her.

"You really like this girl," Bix observed from underneath Elijah's truck one afternoon as they were changing the oil. Earnest sat nearby on the steps of the back porch, he'd never changed oil in a car in his life.

"I do man, she's smart and funny in this really weird way."

"I told you. I know that voice, man," Earnest antagonized.

Elijah rolled his eyes as Bix slid from under the car to look at him.

"Elijah, you *really* like this girl."

"You said that already Bix."

"Yeah, I just never thought I'd be saying it about you. I'm repeating it until it feels real," Bix said, only half kidding.

"You've been hanging out with your wife too much. You're starting to sound like her."

"Trust me, if you were having this conversation with Rae there'd be much more squealing involved." Elijah and Earnest laughed at the truth of his statement.

"She's great, it's just..." Elijah stopped himself.

"Uh oh, here it comes," Earnest quipped.

Bix stood to take a swig from his soda bottle, "Just what?"

"Nothing, it's nothing."

Bix narrowed his eyes in suspicion and probed, "She's great, but...," he extended his hand for Elijah to finish his sentence but Elijah ignored the gesture. Earnest, however, began to understand.

"Oh, I get it. You guys have been going out for a while and you still haven't..." Earnest raised his eyebrows to finish the sentence.

"Am I a jerk for bringing that up? I mean she's amazing and beautiful but it's been like two months."

"And?" Bix stated squarely.

"I knew I was talking to the wrong person about this," Elijah said.

"Actually I think you might be talking to the right one this time, I'm not sure your perceived problem has anything to do with the length of time you've been dating." Bix offered.

Earnest and Bix looked at each other and Earnest's mouth opened slowly with a loud "Oh." The light bulb had just turned on. Elijah glared at Bix refusing to understand.

"So you're saying there is no way Elijah's getting any until they're married?" Earnest asked for Elijah, goading a little.

"Who is they? We've been dating for like five minutes and you've already got us walking down the aisle?" There was a little panic in his voice. "Besides Bix, nobody does that anymore," Elijah said, still in denial.

Bix's face tightened as he leaned deeply to one side. "That is not entirely true, *most* people may not, but some still do."

"Wow man, it's like you're dating a unicorn or a fairy," Earnest mused out loud.

"I did," a voice chimed from behind them. They turned to find Elsa Rae walking out from the house carrying more sodas. Bix smiled before lowering his head to return to work on the car.

All of a sudden Elijah's mouth felt dry and his stomach lurched. *I am not having this conversation with my little sister and her husband.* He covered his ears with his hands and began to talk over them.

"I'm really sorry I brought it up let's not talk about it anymore," he yelled as if at a rock concert.

"Really dude how old are you? Four?" Earnest yelled back from the porch step.

Elsa Rae shook her head, "Ok, ok I get it." Pulling his hand from his ear, Elsa continued, "this topic is off limits for us, but you should at least talk to Molly about it."

Elijah made a face of disgust before burying his head in the hood of the car.

"Alright," Earnest changed the subject, "my lunch break's over and I gotta get back. My boss is this crazy task master!"

"Dinner on Sunday." Elsa reminded him. Earnest nodded in compliance before kissing her on the cheek.

Once Earnest was gone Elsa Rae looked at Bix and then addressed Elijah, "We actually have an abrupt change of subject we think you might like better anyway."

Elijah looked up from the hood of the car to see Bix and Elsa smiling at each other. He turned to give them his full attention, curious.

"How do you feel about being an uncle?" Bix asked nonchalantly.

Elijah looked at Elsa Rae, who was beaming. He ran toward her and swept her up in a hug. When he finally set her down he made his way to Bix and gave him a handshake before pulling him in for a hug as well.

<hr>

The Wednesday afternoon lull was torture. Elijah took advantage of the quiet and decided to take some of the empty boxes to the dumpster as an excuse to get out in the sun. He and Molly had plans later that evening and only half of his mind was on work. The other half was lost in the thought of Molly's arms around him and the smell of her as he hugged her hello. It was the only thing getting him through the viciously mundane day. On his way back from the dumpster he spotted Earnest in back of the shop sitting on an empty crate staring at nothing. Elijah had seen that look before. It was loss. He'd seen it stretched across Jim's face when he accidentally walked in on him in the office one day a few months after Percey had passed. Elijah had been more startled than Jim and the look on Jim's face haunted him long after that moment. It was more than just sadness, Jim looked lost. And now, so did Earnest.

"Earnest?" Elijah pulled up another crate and sat beside his friend. Earnest looked up slowly, as though his mind had been a million miles away.

"What happened man?" Elijah asked.

"It's over," Earnest whispered almost to himself.

"What's over?"

"Everything," he peered up at Elijah, broken.

Earnest explained that the firm he worked for had gotten involved in some shady business with an even shadier client. Everything about the new case was shrouded in secrets so when Earnest stumbled upon proof of wrongdoing, he quietly took it to one of the partners. Apparently it hadn't been quiet enough and when Earnest expressed his reluctance to continue work on the case the higher ups quickly assumed, *if you're not with us you're against us.* He was dismissed from the firm and blacklisted in the city.

Earnest had set things in motion for a wrongful termination suit before he left Atlanta, but had just gotten word that the firm was threatening to counter sue for breach of contract considering his non-disclosure agreement. On top of everything else, they claimed Earnest had shared privileged information and they were moving for him to be disbarred.

All of his dreams since the age of twelve were being swept away because he wanted to do the right thing. He loved being a lawyer, not for the suits or lifestyle but because he loved the law. Earnest loved what the law could help people accomplish. He believed in justice and truth and all those sappy things men of honor could so easily believe in. Elijah had been jealous of that, Earnest's ability to believe. Was this the reward for his belief? Fired, mocked, and banished from the only dream he'd ever had. It seemed it couldn't get worse, until it did.

"I'm sorry Elijah, I just can't sell you the shop."

Elijah said nothing. There were too many words, too many feelings and they all came at once. If he said anything it would be all the wrong things.

"The condo's already been sold, along with my car. I have no job, no hope of getting one, as a lawyer anyway. Right now the shop is all I have."

No, the shop is all I have. For Elijah, there was no condo to sell and no one wanted his car but him. *Selfish!* Elijah wanted to scream at him. It wasn't like Earnest didn't have money, he'd been saving since he was sixteen. By now he surely had enough for several years' worth of rainy days. Deep down though, Elijah knew that what Earnest lost had nothing to do with money. He had lost his identity. But why couldn't he see that by holding on to the shop he was taking that same thing from Elijah?

"Nothing would really change..." Earnest started, afraid of the coldness making its way onto Elijah's face.

Elijah had been there the summer Earnest first discovered girls. He knew all the secrets of his first kiss with Marian Harper, who always whipped them both in basketball. Elijah had been the one who stood up for him when Henry Logan waited outside the band room to pummel him. Now, here they were sitting across from each other, complete strangers—worse than strangers, enemies. Not because of how they felt for each other, but because they both needed the same thing with the same desperation.

"You would still run the store I'd just be here to help more..." Earnest tried to soften the blow, but they both knew it was a lie. Everything would change. Everything had already changed.

Elijah stood up and left without a word. Earnest called to him but Elijah could barely hear him. He walked through the shop and out of the front door. He kept walking, certain that if he stopped, even for a moment, everything he was feeling would swallow him whole. So he walked and let his thoughts march past, never resting on any one for too long.

He didn't realize how long he'd been walking until his phone rang. It was Molly. She was probably wondering why he was late for their date. He couldn't find the energy to talk to her right now. He couldn't talk to anyone. Elijah was angry with Earnest Jay but for a moment he thought of him, how his face looked when he admitted out loud that his dream was gone, solemn and pitiable. Elijah quickly shoved the sympathy back down and the wave of fury returned. All he could think about was how much he had let Jim down, how angry he was with Earnest Jay, and how empty his future looked without the promise of owning the shop. He realized now how reckless it had been to put so much of who he was into one thing. He hadn't lost a store; he'd lost a legacy. He felt the last of Jim was slipping away and all he knew was that he never wanted to feel loss this way again. He tried to think of something else, anything else.

Molly looked at her phone for what seemed like the one hundredth time. It had only been a few seconds since the last time she looked but maybe there was some sort of time vortex, or maybe her phone was still on silent and she'd missed the call but gained a voicemail. It was unlike Elijah to be late, it was almost impossible that he would stand her up. It just wasn't who he was. He was dependable, even if he had to cancel he would call to tell her. Wouldn't he? The only reason he wouldn't call was if something happened. She stopped herself abruptly. *You're spinning out.* She picked up her keys and headed for the door, determined to prove there was nothing to be afraid of.

On the drive to Elijah's, Molly couldn't decide if she was angry or worried. When she got to his house and there was no car in the drive she settled firmly on worried. She decided not to drag Elsa or Bix into it just yet. She could still hear Elsa's voice that morning she showed up at her house after the storm, all panic and anger. She couldn't do that to her again, especially now that she was pregnant. It just seemed wise to keep her fears to herself.

It was almost eleven when Elijah finally pulled up in the driveway. When he got out of his car he seemed annoyed to find her there waiting on him. He nodded in her direction but said nothing as he walked into the house leaving the main door open for her while the screen door bounced closed. Her mood shifted quickly and Molly's worry morphed into fury. She gathered herself and slowly entered the apartment, ready for a fight.

Elijah had already started on his first beer and he avoided her gaze when she entered. He muttered something about her not needing to come all this way. Her eyes narrowed.

"Stop."

He didn't like the command or that there had been one. He didn't like the way the calmness of her voice made him feel, like he had been doing something wicked.

"What happened to you?" Her frustration apparent.

There was no malice or anger in her wide eyes, but he could tell she was hurt. He hated this feeling too, like he owed her something. He didn't want to owe anyone anything, it was why he'd spent the last three hours walking and then driving, aimlessly. She was asking for a confession that he simply was not strong enough to give, even to himself. He wanted her to go away, to stop making him feel.

"I can't do this with you right now," he said brushing past her and walking towards the door.

"Elijah," she demanded. He had never heard his name like that from her before. She was reprimanding him, with his own name. "I just spent hours waiting for you, worried about you."

He imagined her pacing in the driveway, pulling apart the curls in her thick black hair with her thumb and index finger, the way she did when she was nervous or focused on something. But the image made him feel too much so he pushed that away too.

"Sorry, I should have called," he offered half-heartedly.

"I don't want your apologies, Elijah, I want an explanation!"

It was the loudest he'd heard her since the night of the storm. Lately the only loud thing between them was laughter. He didn't like hurting her.

"Earnest is keeping the shop."

It was quiet as if saying it had been an accident. Molly's face didn't change. No sympathy or even anger, she just watched him.

Unable to stand the heat of her glare he continued out onto the stairs with his beer and sat down. When the screen door opened a few minutes later he was sure it was Molly's exit. Instead, she sat on the stairs next to him. She wrapped her arms around her knees and drew them close to her. He knew what she was doing, she was going to try and make things better with a host of catch phrases and well wishes, but he wasn't in the mood.

"I don't want to talk," he warned in a low rumble.

She stared into the darkness in front of her, "Then don't."

She turned to him for a moment to make sure he understood what she was offering him then turned again to face the night. He did understand. She was saying, *I don't care if you're broken, so long as you let me see who you really are.* In that moment, in the dark silence, Elijah admitted to himself that the length of time didn't matter, he would wait with this woman just as she was willing to wait with him.

Elijah was making the finishing touches on his dish when Widow Liddell knocked at his door.

"Happy Thanksgiving," he offered cheerfully as he invited her in, but Elijah could tell she'd come to discuss more than just his holiday plans.

"Is everything alright?" He asked, hoping to give her an easy way into the conversation.

"Yes, everything is fine, it's just..." she paused, "the little dark girl who has been over here recently... you two aren't..." she couldn't finish the question and Elijah was glad because it meant that on some level she understood the absurdity of what was coming out of her mouth.

"Dating? Yes ma'am. We are."

"Oh," she said in that incredibly disapproving tone that only mothers and grandmothers possess.

Elijah tore a page from his mother and Ma Eloise's handbook and decided to kill her with kindness. "I'd love to introduce you sometime."

"Of course, of course. It's just...be careful dear. I know how young love is, it's all so overwhelming in the beginning, but just make sure that you're thinking about the long run too. At your age you want to date the kind of girl you can build a life with."

He countered her insult, "I couldn't agree with you more."

"Well I'd better get back to my greens. I have a house full of people coming over for dinner."

Elijah wasted no time ushering her to the door. He didn't notice Molly on the very last step until the widow reached the bottom and the two exchanged glances. Molly had heard her. Widow Liddell knew and felt no remorse. The awkwardness was palpable but Widow Liddell maintained her Southern disposition in lieu of politeness. She gave Molly a tight-lipped smile, which Molly never returned, then walked across the yard to her house.

Elijah hoped in vain that Molly hadn't heard their conversation. He knew the widow was a harmless old-fashioned gossip who was well-meaning but firmly grounded in the 1950's. He'd hoped that Molly wasn't fazed by the silly old woman's ignorance but when she reached the top of the stairs to greet him she could barely manage a smile. He realized it wasn't that simple for her.

Molly understood something that Elijah didn't. She recognized Widow Liddell as the most dangerous of all racists because she truly believed what she was saying. It was the sincerity of her belief that made her a threat.

Thanksgiving dinner at Ma Eloise's was just what they needed to lighten the mood. Since the death of their mother, Ma Eloise and the Hargros had become Elsa and Elijah's family. Even Bix preferred Thanksgiving dinner at Ma Eloise's to his own mother's. There was something about the way the Hargro house was always so full of warmth and life. Even the game day trash talk seemed welcoming. The world outside may have been treacherous and strange, but inside these walls

Elijah and Elsa always felt safe. The smell of pies and cakes filled the whole house till it poured out into the driveway. They could always smell dessert long before they ever reached the front door.

Molly, Elsa, and Ma Eloise buzzed around the kitchen laughing, joking, and talking. Elijah popped in under the false pretense of needing another drink but no one even noticed he was in the room. He eased into the kitchen, shifted Elsa from in front of the refrigerator to grab a soda, kissed Ma Eloise as he passed her, then winked at Molly who was on the other side of the counter before ducking back out of the kitchen. Molly's eyes lingered after him for a second too long, when she turned to face Eloise and Elsa they were beaming at her. Molly attempted to cover her embarrassment by starting the conversation again.

Her gracious friend obliged, "I think we're almost ready to start dinner!"

"Ok, I guess I'll make a plate for Elijah before the crowd starts."

Elsa and Ma Eloise looked back at her again.

"I'm sorry, is there a rule about who gets food first?" Molly apologized.

"No. It's just we're not really used to Elijah dating the kind of girl who fixes his plate," Elsa offered.

"It's just food. None of the girls he brought home before thought he might want to eat?"

Ma Eloise couldn't help letting out a little laugh, "What girls?"

Elsa huffed a little, "He's only brought one other girl home."

"She was definitely not the plate-fixing type," Ma Eloise added.

Molly couldn't help smiling as she made her way to the dishes laid out on the counter.

"Food is ready," Elsa sang from the doorway of the kitchen. The family immediately started to stir. Elijah made his way towards the kitchen when Elsa put her hand on his arm to stop him. He was about to complain when he looked up to find Molly exiting the kitchen, a plate in each hand. His mouth opened a little and he looked back at Elsa as if to find something to say. She smiled and winked at him before turning her attention to the rest of the guests.

Elijah reached to help Molly then made room for her on the couch next to him. "You didn't have to do that," Elijah objected although he was completely enchanted. Who was this woman and where had she come from?

"I figured it was the only way to secure food for both of us. I've been taste-testing all afternoon and I don't think there would have been anything left if we waited," Molly brushed off the thanks.

He drew her in and kissed her on the temple.

"I see we done lost another one," Jordan, Ma Eloise's great nephew, said to his cousin, Eric, loud enough for everyone to hear.

Eric laughed, but quietly. Earnest Jay, always one for an entrance, made his way through the front door just in time to notice Molly's smile dissolve. She shifted uncomfortably in her seat and Earnest paused instinctively in order to keep out of whatever he had just walked in on. Elijah hadn't realized that the comment was offensive, but Molly's reaction made him feel as though he should have.

"Lost another what?" Elijah asked discerning her mood. Jordan looked over and noticed Molly's face, then Elijah's. Earnest began to understand, slowly.

"Ah, nothing man. I was just playing."

Jordan's reaction made Elijah even more aware that he had been mocking them. He didn't like it.

"No really, lost another what?" This time the question sounded more like a challenge.

"It's fine Elijah," Molly soothed him resting her hand against his chest. "I think Jordan just meant that he missed out on another amazing woman now that I'm dating you."

The room tightened with the truth, and everyone strained to hear what would come next. Elijah's jaw tightened in anger, but also in fear. He didn't know how to defend her from this. He seemed unqualified to have this fight, so he just sat still waiting to follow her lead.

"Jordan, let me ask you a question," Molly started, affecting her best lawyer impression.

Earnest shushed the busy bodies around him to hear what came next.

"I lived here for almost six months before I started dating Elijah. Why didn't you ever ask me out?"

Silence filled the room and everyone's heads turned to see Jordan's reaction. There was something in Jordan's eyes that reminded her of her brother when he used to get in trouble. There was a little shame yes, but underneath was resentment for being called out on something. Something that bellowed, *how dare you be right about me!*

"Cause he's a punk," Eric answered for him after the silence had lingered just a moment too long.

Earnest and everyone else in earshot exploded with laughter, including Molly. Even Jordan cracked a small smile.

"Well, man up next time so you don't miss out," Molly continued the playful mockery.

Eric walked over to her and held out his fist. She bumped it with her own before looking up at him. He winked to reassure her. Ma Eloise entered and the room grew quiet, everyone knew what came next. They laid down their plates and joined hands.

Everyone looked up at Ma Eloise, but she turned to Jordan, "Baby, why don't you lead us. You can pray for a little courage for yourself too."

Everyone roared with laughter again and Jordan took his family's jabs like a pro boxer. They lowered their heads and gave thanks with hearts light from laughter.

Elijah exhaled before realizing he was even holding his breath. It hadn't occurred to him how much this family's opinion meant to him. With Katy it had been so important for her to treat them well that he hadn't thought to worry about how *they* might treat someone else. Molly belonged with this family, even if she didn't fit. Not because of how she looked, but because of who she was. She was just like he and Elsa—a beloved outsider.

Later that night, as things were winding down and the crowd started to dwindle, Elijah's eyes searched the room for Molly. Earnest made his way over to him first.

"So that's her, huh?" He finished putting on his coat then flipped the collar down.

Elijah said nothing, only smiled proudly.

"I knew I was gonna like her," he buttoned his coat, kicked Elijah's shoe then made his way out of the front door. Elijah stood from the couch still grinning and made his way to the kitchen to find Molly. She had disappeared somewhere around the end of the game and Elijah assumed she was helping Elsa or Ma Eloise. Elsa and Bix were in the kitchen, flirting unabashedly with each other. Elsa pointed to the back porch where Molly and Ma Eloise were talking. He liked the way they looked, both comfortable and calm, Molly bouncing her foot while Ma Eloise took a sip of her tea.

"Don't pay her any mind honey," Ma Eloise was saying. "People like that are so worried about how other people look to them, they have no idea how they look to everybody else."

Molly quietly let the words sink in hoping they would calm the waves of emotion stirring inside her. It almost worked, but not quite. Ma Eloise caught sight of Elijah and smiled at him before shifting her weight to stand.

"I'm gonna see if Elsa left me anything to do in there."

"I can help you," Elijah offered.

"No, you stay," she said firmly, giving him a look that let him know he should take up the conversation where she left off.

"What's up?"

"Just thinking," Molly offered, her voice lower than usual.

"About Widow Liddell? Ignore her. That's what I do."

After a few more moments of silence she began, "It's not just her and it's not just what she said. It's that she actually believes that how I look, who I am, makes me somehow morally wrong for you."

"Molly, the thing is, the fact that she thinks that proves how ignorant she is. Everything about who you are makes me better."

She lowered her eyes and Elijah moved to kneel in front of her. "You know what worried me most about tonight?" Molly lifted her eyes to look at him as he continued.

"That we wouldn't fit *here*, with the people who matter most to me. I'm not with you so we can help the world make sense of us," he brushed her chin with his finger before lifting it. "I'm with you because *you* make sense in my world."

Molly wrapped him in her arms and held him there for a long time. They let the silence and the cool night breeze wash over them.

PART III

What We Choose

CHAPTER 13

All We Never Say

Molly was sure they were nearing the end. They'd had a good run. Truth be told, Elijah had opened her heart in ways she didn't even think were still possible for her. But just eight short months after they'd started dating Elijah was drifting away.

He'd cancelled three dinner dates in the past two weeks, he was almost always rushing her off the phone, and even when he was around he was always so distracted. He'd spent the past four nights locked away in his workshop and when she'd asked if he wanted any help he quickly dismissed the offer. "No, thanks I got it."

These warning signs were in addition to the fact that he had never fully recovered from his fallout with Earnest Jay. They were still friends, or at least they were still friendly, but the brotherhood she'd always heard him describe wasn't there anymore.

Was she was losing him to his sadness? It seemed that the more she tried to be there for him, the more he pulled away. Why wouldn't he just end it already?

Maybe he was too afraid to hurt her, or maybe he wasn't man enough to say he was done with her, with them. Either way, Molly was sure the end was coming and she refused to stand by and let it gradually chip away at her. The thought alone was like torture, waiting around for someone to break her heart. Someone who was more than capable, because even if she hadn't admitted it to him, Elijah held such a big part of her heart now. The only thing that scared her more than sticking around for him to break her heart was the thought of breaking his.

What if she was wrong, what if all he really needed from her was more time? Time to sort things out with Earnest or figure out how he felt about her. But how much time would be enough? Maybe someday soon Elijah would be ready, but was she supposed to sit around and wait for that to happen? She had been through the pain of waiting too long before and she wouldn't put herself or Elijah through that again.

"Hey, babe I'm sorry to do this again, but I'm going to have to cancel tonight."

He was in his car with the windows down and Molly could hear the wind whipping around him.

"It's ok," she sighed into her end of the phone.

"No, I'm going to make this up to you I promise," Elijah continued, but Molly could tell he was once again distracted.

She took a deep breath, closed her eyes and ripped off the band-aid, "You don't have to make it up to me Elijah. I think we should just cut our losses."

"Cut our what?" Elijah asked, clearly confused.

"Look, I know things are weird for you at the shop and you're working really hard to get back on track. I don't want to distract you from any of that," Molly continued, eyes still closed with tears forming behind the lids.

"I have no idea what you're talking about right now. Where are you?"

"I'm on my way home."

"Ok, I'll meet you there. I'm on my way." Elijah turned the wheel of his car to head in her direction. He didn't like the way her voice sounded. She seemed tired or scared, but he couldn't tell without seeing her eyes. He needed to see what was wrong with her.

"No. Elijah, I'm on my way home to my parents' house, in Atlanta."

Elijah froze. *Atlanta? Why?*

"Molly what are you saying?"

The wind had stopped and she could tell he wasn't driving anymore. Her face was full of tears now, but she steadied her voice.

"I'm saying it was selfish of me to try and hold on to you when you have so much going on. I should have given you space when you asked for it, but I'm giving it to you now." The last few words were barely audible.

"Molly," was all he could get out. He didn't know what to say. He wasn't even sure what was happening. Was she ending them? Was she taking away the one beautiful thing he had left? Why? There had to be something else to say, something to keep her on the line longer, something to make her change her mind. For the life of him he couldn't figure out what that something was. Then, all of a sudden it was too late.

"Goodbye Elijah." The line went silent.

He sank back in the driver's seat of his truck and watched the tassel from the "World's Greatest Uncle" charm that Elsa made him dangle from the rear view mirror.

"What just happened," he wondered out loud.

"What happened?"

Elsa Rae continued to pry over lunch a few days later despite her husband's repeated throat clearing. It seemed that when the seventh month of pregnancy passed so did all inclination to take hints or advice. All of a sudden she was more adventurous than she'd ever been. Her present state made some of her explorations impossible, but she was definitely taking advantage of the ones she could. Some worked in Bix's favor, but this new found outspokenness did not.

"Elsa, we've already talked about this," Elijah said into his plate.

"No we didn't," she retorted with the indifference of a toddler, "I keep asking and you keep changing the subject."

"Maybe that means he doesn't want to talk about it, sweetheart," Bix offered quietly.

"Well, did you at least talk to *her* about it?"

Elijah looked up at her, ready to explode, but stopped himself because her eyes were shining with so much hope. She really wanted to fix this. He could see how much it meant to her. He wanted to fix it too, but you can't fix something when you don't know where the problem is and Molly hadn't given him enough time to figure that out.

"She doesn't want to talk Rae. And neither do I." He said it quietly, but firmly.

Elsa Rae's curiosity was not yet satisfied, but she could see the conversation was over so she pushed back her chair and began reaching for dishes. Bix was still working on his last bite as she lifted his plate from the table. Elijah had lost his appetite, as was evident by the piles of food left on his plate. Elsa reached across the table to grab his plate and Elijah looked up to thank her, but her face was twisted in discomfort.

"Rae, you ok?" he asked.

She opened her mouth to dismiss his concern when her face contorted again. This time Bix noticed too, he scrambled to his feet and lowered her into her chair. She wasn't reaching for her stomach, but the area just below it. She didn't look like she was in pain really, just uncomfortable, like hitting a funny bone. Bix, ever the overprotective husband, was not willing to take any chances and despite her protestations when the discomfort subsided a few minutes later, Bix insisted they pay the doctor a visit.

"He was overreacting wasn't he?" Elsa teased as the doctor finished up the exam.

Dr. Lamont, a beautiful Panamanian woman in her early fifties, smiled sweetly.

"There is no such thing when it comes to the safety of your baby," she said sincerely, but with a hint of *this happens all the time.*

"See, overreacting," Elsa mocked her husband who was shaking his head at her playfully.

"But..."

It's funny that such a small word could make a room go quiet so quickly.

"But what?" Bix worried.

"It's nothing for you two to worry about. Baby is growing big and strong in there," she eased into the issue.

Elsa Rae didn't want to be handled, "But what?" She seconded her husband's question, only with far less patience.

"Because of the baby's size and activity, there is a little more wear and tear on your pelvis than I'd like to see." The doctor took off her gloves and slid back in her chair so that she could look at them both at the same time.

"I just want to make sure that both mommy and baby stay safe, so I'm going to put you on bed rest and strict pelvic rest for the remainder of the pregnancy." She looked intently at Bix with raised eyebrows. Elsa and Bix both laughed like teenagers caught making out.

"But everything's ok with the baby right?" Elsa urged.

"Baby is doing great." Dr. Lamont assured them.

They didn't know they'd been holding their breath, but the sigh after the good news was proof enough.

"And you still don't want to know the sex of the baby right?" Dr. Lamont asked.

"Right," they chimed together. There were lots of things they didn't agree on, but they were completely in sync on not knowing the sex of their first born. The decision was driving the future grandparents a little crazy. Ma Eloise and Bix's mother had been complaining nonstop about not being able to shop more specifically for their new grandbaby, but the parents held firm.

"Alright then, I guess we're all done here." Dr. Lamont said as she stood.

After Elsa and Bix left for the doctor, Elijah was alone again, restless and trapped with his own thoughts. He headed back to the shop to get some work done. He was hard at work on a restoration. Mr. Thompson had brought in an antique sideboard his wife found at an antique shop in Maine over the winter. It hadn't been appraised yet, but Elijah could tell from the style it was probably made in the early 1900's and definitely American. It was beautiful, functional, classic. He'd taken one look at it and knew how much fun he would have restoring it. It was sturdy and strong, but needed a lot of work. The former owner tried to make some "improvements" but the piece was worse off as a result. It took Elijah nearly two months just to find the original hardware and another month to find the right oak to replace a broken panel. It was starting to come together and Elijah was proud of his work. He'd spent the last few days stripping the sideboard and he wanted to finish that part of the project before morning.

He slipped off his jacket and slid his fingers across the top of the sideboard. He loved furniture, loved this shop, the way it smelled and how quiet it got at night. The shop smelled like Jim, like how Elijah remembered him, wood, sawdust, tobacco, and sweat. His whole adolescence was wrapped up in this place and with every breath he could sense how much he'd grown up here.

He'd actually spent a lot of nights here since he and Molly had been dating. He suspected it had something to do with the vigor required to work on large pieces. No sex was a noble idea, but much harder to put into action. With every passing month it became more and more clear to Elijah that Bix was right about Molly waiting. They'd never talked about it, but at this point it was understood. Sort of like Elijah's feelings about the shop, or Earnest for that matter, it was there, but they didn't bring it up.

Elijah had discovered that working was the best way to burn energy, or clear his mind, or dream if he wanted. But tonight was different, for the first time in eight months Elijah didn't have the silent satisfaction of knowing someone was thinking of him, waiting on him, wanting him. Tonight it was just he and the sideboard, until it wasn't anymore.

Elijah sat down and pulled a beer from the cooler near the craft table where his tools hung and as he pulled the bottle up to his lips he saw Earnest's shadow—looming, sad, ominous. Wasn't there a single place in this town where he could find some peace? He quickly took a swig of his beer, put it down and picked up his sand paper. He hoped that if Earnest saw him hard at work he'd take a hint. He didn't.

"Hey," Earnest muttered.

Elijah lifted his head slightly in reply. Earnest brushed off the halfhearted greeting and picked up some sand paper. Elijah fumed silently and continued his work.

"Where's honey bee?"

Elijah stared blankly at him.

"It's what the guys call Molly."

Elijah fought off a smile. Honey bee, Molly would love that.

"Went home to see her family," Elijah mumbled without looking up from his work.

"Is this how it's going to be now," Earnest asked. He was calm, but Elijah could sense the storm that was coming.

"How what's going to be?" Elijah rose to take another swig of beer. Earnest glared at him.

"You know what Elijah, if you want to sit around hiding in your fort pouting like a little girl go right ahead," Earnest tossed the sand paper and headed towards the door.

Elijah stood from his stool, livid. "Little girl? Who came home and sulked for months without so much as a word about why you were here? You never even would have come clean about keeping the shop if I hadn't dragged it out of you."

"I was trying to fix it!"

"Fat lot of good it did us both, huh?"

"You know what Elijah, forget you. I lost everything! Everything I own, everything I am. Do you get that? Do you even know what that means?" Earnest shouted moving closer to him.

Elijah took a step back, he didn't want to hurt Earnest, but if he took another step towards him he was definitely going to.

"How *would* you know? Everything you ever wanted, you got." Earnest moved closer to Elijah with each word.

He must have been drunk. Earnest had never won a fight against Elijah in his life. Not even a playful wrestling match.

"Every girl, any job, this shop!" Earnest came closer still and Elijah's hand closed tightly into a fist.

"You could never know what it's like to—"

Elijah shut him up with a fist to his jaw and Earnest stumbled back. A calmer, more sober Earnest would have known his limits. He would have seen that Elijah could have ended this fight with two more punches. But drunk Earnest believed he was a gladiator. If this fight was to the death, so be it. He spat blood and landed a swift right to Elijah's eye. Instinctively Elijah lifted his hand to it, the flesh around his eye was warm and throbbing. Earnest felt this small victory too deeply and Elijah wasted no time landing a solid punch to Earnest's gut. When he folded forward in pain, Elijah leaned in and hissed, "You have no idea what I lost!"

Enraged, Earnest lunged at him forcing him into the sideboard. Fists flew and one piece of furniture after another took blows.

All the things they were fighting finally had a face and they fought with all their strength. But they weren't sixteen-year old boys sparring in the back yard anymore. Nearly killing each other took much more effort than it once did, there was much more pride at stake now. Neither had come this far to give in to something as trivial as age, so with one last burst of energy Earnest ran at Elijah pushing him through a door in the workshop where they collapsed in a breathless heap in front of an elaborate piece of woodwork. They laid on their backs in silence trying to catch their breath. The fight was over, but neither wanted to be the first to admit it. That would be admitting defeat. There had to be something they could talk about instead. From his back Earnest looked up above his head and saw the woodwork.

"What's that?" Earnest asked with much more breath than words. Elijah turned to see what he was looking at then turned back and rested his head on the ground.

"Porch swing for Molly."

"Oh. It's nice."

The two broken men rested on the sideboard each with a beer in his hand. There was no use trying to be respectful now, the sideboard had taken a few hard hits in the scuffle. Elijah was sure it was going to need twice the work it had when Thompson brought it in. Elijah shrugged it off. He'd fix it, stall with Mr. and Mrs. Thompson, and then discount them for the extra time. There were also two broken antique chairs, and a table that suffered in the great struggle. The damage was minor, but would still require time he didn't have. Fighting as a grown man seemed more trouble than it was worth. But he did feel better and, judging by Earnest's whimsical use of his beer bottle as an ice pack, so was he.

"So why haven't you given your girl the swing yet," Earnest asked before bringing the bottle to one side of his mouth to avoid touching the side of his lip that was busted and bleeding.

"She's not my girl anymore," Elijah said evenly. The punching and beers had made it easier to say, but apparently not any easier for Earnest to hear.

"Come on man, don't tell me that! What'd you do?"

Elijah laughed, not offended in the least. He was almost certain it was his fault too, he just wished he knew what "it" was.

"I don't know man," he mumbled into his beer.

"Does she even know about it?" he pointed to the swing.

"No," he answered matter-of-factly. *And she's not going to. Exes don't get refurbished antique porch swings,* he thought to himself.

"So what are you going to do with it now?" Earnest pressed.

"Probably sell it. It's a nice piece, I could probably get about a thousand for it."

"A thousand dollars?" He almost choked on his beer.

"I don't know why you hanging around here fixing stuff when you can make something worth a thousand dollars," Earnest mused before taking another drink.

Elijah laughed it off but there was a feeling in the pit of his stomach, a feeling very close to the one he'd gotten that first day he spoke to Jim in the park. It felt close to hope, but was much more like destiny.

"But you know you're never going to see that thousand dollars right?" Earnest prodded.

"Why not," Elijah asked defiantly.

"Cause you're not gonna sell it."

"Watch," Elijah said arrogantly.

Earnest stopped and turned towards him, "Elijah, come on man. I told you this girl was for you before I even knew her."

"Exactly, you don't know her."

"But I know you," Earnest replied, and there didn't seem to be a comeback for that response.

"You love her man, and whether she's confused or frustrated or whatever, she loves you too," Elijah pretended not to listen, pressing the bottle to his lips again.

Earnest stood to leave, "Put that porch swing in the back of that raggedy truck and go get your girl."

Elijah let out a sad laugh. Earnest walked towards the door but halted and turned to him.

"Elijah, about before," Earnest started sincerely.

"Yeah, me too," Elijah finished.

They shared a quick head nod and without a word the feud ended. With Earnest gone the quiet returned, and with it questions. He had so many questions and all of them about Molly. He needed them answered, every single one, and right now.

Molly was asleep when the buzz of her phone woke her. She was annoyed at first. Sleep had been hard to come by these days. She wasn't crying as much anymore but at night when her mind was quiet all she could think about was Elijah. How she missed him, how she'd hurt him, how much she didn't want to be hurt.

The text message read, "Come outside." Her heart nearly beat her down the stairs it was pounding so hard. What was Elijah doing here and how did he even know where here was? *Elsa,* she realized as she descended the stairs. Molly had given Elsa her parent's address so she could mail her baby shower invitation. She knew it had been a ruse when Elsa asked for it. Molly had been planning the shower with her for a month and didn't need an invitation. She knew the real reason Elsa wanted the address she just never expected Elijah to actually use it.

"Hi," Molly said as she opened the door.

It was dark so she couldn't yet see the bruises that were starting to develop on his face. A moment later, she gasped, "What happened?"

She reached for him, too worried to be nervous anymore. She touched his cheek gently, afraid she would hurt him if she applied any pressure. Her fingers felt like feathers on his skin and he missed her so much it ached. He wanted to hold her, but he steadied himself, this wasn't what he came for.

"Why'd you break up with me?"

"What?" She pulled her hand away from his face instinctively.

"You broke up with me. Why?"

The question was straight and stiff and offered no soft places or corners to hide in, but that didn't stop Molly from trying. She stared at her feet. One was on top of the other and she was moving the toes of one foot along the top of the other.

"Molly," Elijah called a little more loudly than he intended. She quickly shushed him then put her hand on his chest to push him out of the front door. She pulled her robe closed and held it tightly, but it wasn't cold. It wasn't the air she was trying to keep out, it was him.

"Why did you…"

"Because I thought it was what you wanted!"

Elijah's brow creased and he took a step back.

"You thought I wanted you to break up with me over the phone for no apparent reason at all?" He could see the wheels turning in her mind and for the first time it occurred to him that Molly may not know why they broke up either.

"You weren't calling and you kept pulling away and I just thought you needed space because of the thing with the shop." She was rambling and nervous, she couldn't even look at him. "I just…I didn't want to be in your way."

He put his finger under her chin and pulled her face upward. "I like you in my way."

She smiled, her eyes back on her feet now.

"Come here."

He took her hand and led her to the back of the truck, lifting a tarp to reveal the swing. Even when he was loading the swing he didn't know why he felt he needed to cover it. It was like he was protecting it, protecting her.

"What is this?"

"It's a swing for your porch."

She looked at him with her eyes wide then turned back to the swing.

"You said you wanted one," he finished.

She was quiet and still and he couldn't see her face from where she was standing. *She doesn't like it,* he reprimanded himself. Earnest would have mocked him for this, "where is that thousand dollar swagger now?" Elijah was so distracted by her silence that it took him a moment to notice her shoulders shaking.

"Are you crying?"

She didn't say anything. She just stood trying to make her body still. When she took in another breath the sound betrayed her and Elijah turned her around to face him. Her face was full of tears and her hands were clasped so gracefully in front of her mouth that it looked like she was praying.

"I love it," she exhaled. "Thank you."

Elijah pulled her into his chest and held her there. He still didn't understand what all of this meant or why she was so afraid, but this was better, at least now they were confused together.

Later that night in the quiet of her parents' basement Molly told Elijah about Clinton, about waiting in vain for him. She hadn't realized, until she saw the swing, just how scared she was that waiting for Elijah would end the same way. With Clinton it hadn't mattered as much, losing him was inconvenient, but not heartbreaking. With Elijah it was different, she didn't just want him to stay, she needed *him* to want to stay.

"I think that's why I never talk about sex with you either." She blurted.

He had wanted so badly to talk to her about this all the way up until the moment they were actually talking about it. Molly saw his face and laughed. She covered his chin and mouth with her hand and pushed it away. He smiled before grabbing her hand and kissing it.

"So we're actually about to have this conversation?" He said into her hand.

"Sure, why not," she shrugged, exhausted from all the crying.

"Ok, so you're..." he started, afraid to hear the answer.

"Waiting until I'm married to have sex. Yes," she answered, straight, no self-righteousness, no soap box, just the truth.

"Just, rip the band aid right off, huh?" He liked her like this, relaxed and honest.

She laughed aloud and this time it was he who shushed her. She covered her mouth quickly.

"So, I mean, you're sure about this? There's no changing your mind," he teased.

She was still smiling, but she much more serious, "I'm sure."

He turned his head to face the ceiling then nodded. "Why didn't you just tell me this before?"

Molly leaned her head and pursed her lips. "Do you even remember our first date? You were like the rogue cowboy."

Elijah recalled the old flames they ran into that first night at Lilly's and laughed. Part of him liked that she thought of him that way, dangerous and sexy.

"Add that to the fact that you already had one foot out the door in the first place," she continued.

"Whoa, whoa, whoa. Low blow, that's not fair," he said, more wounded than he cared to admit.

"Elijah! Are you kidding me? If we weren't stuck in that house together every day you probably would have bailed after the first time I called you out." It was true, as much as he hated to own it.

It occurred to him that she'd spent most of their time together listening, avoiding talking. Even though what she thought made him uncomfortable, he was grateful to have her share it with him.

"Well I'm really glad we were stuck in that house together every day then," he said pulling her closer to him by her calf.

"Hmm," she hummed

When she was close enough he rested his forehead on hers. "I'm not going anywhere," he whispered to her.

She hung her hands from the back of his neck to pull him closer. "You promise?"

She was smiling, but he could hear her voice trembling again. How had he never realized how afraid she was? He had always thought of her as a strong woman. She never seemed to need anyone. But in the safety of her parents' basement she had let him see just how fragile she actually was, she did need. She needed him. He held her face in his hands and lifted it so her eyes met his.

"I promise."

She kissed him deeply then sunk so that her head rested on his chest. He kissed the top of her head and as he drifted back onto the arm of the couch he whispered, "I love you."

She lifted her head to look at him. "I love you too," she whispered before turning away again.

"You're not going to cry again are you?" He joked with his eyes closed.

She punched him in the gut, and the memory of his fisticuffs earlier came rushing to the front of his mind with the pain. Despite the suffering he couldn't help but laugh. He knew there were a few tears on her cheeks already.

"I'm so sick of just sitting here. Let me do *something*," Elsa Rae whined from her bed.

"You know what the doctor said, strict bed rest," Bix said, as sweetly as he could. The bed rest had been difficult for Elsa, but apparently it was doing wonders for the baby who was growing heavier and moving more every day. Elsa was happy to know that her child was healthy but she was secretly a little resentful about being rendered incapacitated in the process.

The House We Built

Although he would never admit it, Bix was as sick of the doctor's orders as she was. He never truly understood how much work Elsa Rae did at home and at the nursery until he had to do both of their jobs. Not to mention that his sweet doting wife had turned into a demanding, angry hermit. Stress was piling by the moment and even with Elijah and Molly's help, things were getting harder to manage.

Fortunately, his thoughts were interrupted when Molly entered the bedroom, arms full and smile bright.

"I'm ready for girl's night!"

"Thank God," Bix sighed. He clasped his hands as if in prayer and mouthed *thank you* to Molly. He quickly kissed his wife and made a break for it.

Molly handed Elsa Rae a box of Junior Mints then headed over to cue up the movie. Since the pregnancy Elsa's taste had gone from sweet romantic comedy to somewhat violent action. It was one of the only gains for Bix.

"Bless you," Elsa Rae mumbled as she shoved another two pieces of candy into her mouth.

Molly laughed "How's baby doing?"

"Baby's great, flipping around like an acrobat in there," Elsa said, half frustrated half proud. Molly smiled.

"I don't see how the baby does it." Elsa rubbed her belly, "There is barely any room left in there. I don't know how I'm going to survive another minute of this."

"I guess that sort of answers my question about how you're doing," Molly said.

"I feel so bad for Bix. It's like the old me was swallowed by a really, really hungry monster."

Molly laughed and pulled her friend in for a hug.

Without letting go, Elsa broke the comfortable silence, "How are you and my brother doing?"

Molly couldn't help but roll her eyes, Elsa was so transparent. "We're fine. Actually, Elijah's taking me to dinner next weekend to some fancy restaurant in Atlanta."

Elsa popped up from the hug like a jack-in-the-box, "Really?"

Molly laughed again, "Yes, really, he says it's our official back together dinner."

"But you've been back together for over a month now," Elsa stated, almost like a question.

"Yeah, but we never really did anything to celebrate," Molly answered as she raised the remote to press play on the movie.

"Unless..." Elsa started.

"I'm going to stop you right there. There is no 'unless.' It's just dinner. Let's leave it at that."

"So you *have* thought about it," Elsa accused, pointing.

"I'm a single woman over thirty, Elsa. I thought about it, trust me. But I'm trying not to over think or make a big deal about something that might not be anything. So can we please just watch the movie?"

Elsa Rae relented. She hadn't considered how hard waiting and wondering must be for Molly. She lifted the remote out of Molly's hand and pressed play. They sank into the bed and happily gorged on snacks.

Bix and Elijah got back to the house about eleven o'clock that evening after completing inventory at the nursery. Too exhausted for small talk, Bix tossed Elijah a soda from the refrigerator. Elijah opened the bottle then walked to the bedroom and rested his arm on the frame of the door. He took a sip and when he lowered his head again he smiled as he watched Molly and Elsa Rae asleep in the glow of the television. They were huddled together like sisters who'd been bed mates their whole lives. He smiled at the sight of them, they looked so young. Then he looked at Molly with one arm stretched long underneath her head and the other resting on her waist. Her breathing sounded almost like cooing and Elijah allowed himself to dream of falling asleep to that sound for the rest of his life.

"Hi," he heard a sweet whisper. He drew his mind back from the years it had wandered and saw Molly smiling up at him. He let his head fall to the side and rest on the frame of the door.

"Hi," he said, flirting. Molly was still too groggy to notice.

She pushed herself up to a sitting position and searched the room to gain her bearings. "What time is it?" she asked squinting one eye while trying to focus the other.

Elijah looked down at his watch, "A little after eleven."

"I didn't realize it was so late," she said beginning to gather up her things.

"Come on, I'll drive you home," Elijah said grabbing her bags.

"You don't have to do that, I drove," she answered.

"And risk you falling asleep at the wheel?"

"You make a strong point," she said taking his free hand with one hand and pulling his arm close with the other.

She hugged Bix goodbye assuring him that Elsa Rae was out for the night. He offered his silent gratitude once more then saw them off from the front door.

By the time Elijah got to Molly's she was already sleeping again.

"Babe, babe you're home," he swept her hair from her forehead and tucked it behind her ear. She pretended not to hear him, but they both knew better.

"Molly, sweetheart, I've been lifting plants and soil for the last four hours." She moaned pitifully in reply.

"Sweetheart you're too…"

"Watch it," she warned, but her eyes never opened.

"You're seriously going to make me carry you aren't you?"

She smiled slyly still refusing to open her eyes.

"Fine," he walked around to her side of the car and lifted her out with ease.

He carried her inside and tucked her into her bed, then leaned over her to turn off the light when he heard her voice in his ear.

"Don't drive," she whispered.

She hadn't meant to be, but she was much too close to his ear when she said it. He pulled back for a moment to look at her. She was beautiful. Her thick wavy hair spread out on the pillow, one brown arm resting gracefully on the black wool mass. Her thick lips pursed just slightly, the way they did whenever she was sleepy. He understood now the concept of poetry in motion—her chest rising and falling slowly as she breathed. It was getting harder to wait with her lately. It had been hard in the beginning, Molly was attractive, but now, now that he loved her she seemed the embodiment of beauty and love and sex. More and more since they'd come back from her parent's house he had begun to want not just one thing or the other with her, but everything. He let himself be drawn to her and he parted her lips with his. The kiss woke her and she lazily tossed the arm that had been resting above her behind his neck. He slid his hand under her waist and ran his thumb along her side. They kissed, long and deep. Molly let out a soft sweet sigh and Elijah lowered his head to pull away.

"I don't think that would be a good idea," he whispered still close enough to kiss her. Her eyes slowly opened and she understood.

"You're right," she said smiling.

"The drive would do me some good." He said before kissing her on the nose then the forehead.

He stood to leave and Molly sat up in the bed drawing the covers all the way up to her chin. Elijah turned back at the door and chuckled.

"See you," Molly smiled.

"See you."

CHAPTER 14

A Buck in the Road

Out of the pan and into the fire, was how Elijah had been feeling lately. Since Elsa's forced absence from the nursery he had been taking up slack for her on weekends at Bixby's Bulbs then heading back to Willie's in the evening to finish paperwork and close up for Earnest Jay. Molly had even come in to help out with answering phones and taking orders at both the nursery and the shop, but the trouble was that one was always covering for the other so they barely ever got to see each other or work the same shifts. When Molly showed up unexpectedly at Willie's, Elijah didn't even try to hide his excitement.

"Hey!" He said louder than usual and with one arm already extended to take her by the waist and pull her into his arms.

"Hey," she chirped before giving him a quick peck.

"I brought dinner," she said already making her way to the office.

"I love you!" he said realizing only now that he hadn't eaten anything since breakfast.

"That's what all the hungry boys say," she said only seconds before the office door shut behind her.

An hour and a half later with the last customer gone and the store finally closed, Elijah walked in to find Molly sitting on the front of the desk comforting Earnest Jay who was sitting in the chair with his head lowered.

"What's up, everything ok?" Elijah asked quickly.

"I am officially being sued," Earnest Jay said.

"The firm just called to rub it in his face," Molly continued for him looking up at Elijah with an anger that was so personal and sincere he couldn't remember a time before she was a part of his family.

"But you can still practice law though, that's something. Anyway, I never liked them," Molly asserted.

Elijah smiled, "Sweetheart, you never knew them," he offered gently putting his hand on her shoulder to calm her.

"So! What kind of horrible and immature people call to goad an ex-employee that they just sued? Wrongfully."

At this point, even Earnest had motioned for her to calm down. "Cool down there champ."

Earnest and Elijah shared a quick laugh.

"Sweetheart, is that my food?" Elijah said reaching timidly.

"I hate that we live in a world where people can just do that and get away with it." Molly continued to fume.

"Honey, can I have my..." Elijah said reaching.

"Your what? Oh, no it's cold now." She said still angry, though not at him. She grabbed his dish and stormed out of the office.

"I feel sorry for *all* your children's teachers," Earnest said when he believed Molly was out of earshot.

"Whose children?"

"So, you're going to pretend that you and Molly are not two steps from the altar?"

"What? Do you and Bix have a pool going or something? Everybody just relax. We are enjoying our lives right now and we just got back together." Elijah said his voice a little higher than an honest man's should be.

With the fuss out of the way, Elijah had time to see that Molly had already eaten without him. He looked down at his watch, he hadn't realized how long it had been since she got there.

"A pool is not a bad idea. Tell me when you're going to propose and I'll start one." Earnest Jay continued to tease.

Before Elijah could open his mouth to reply, Molly reentered with Elijah's food. She handed it to him without looking and took her seat on the desk again.

"You know what I was thinking," she said to Earnest Jay with eagerness dripping from each word. He looked up intrigued.

"You know how excited you were about mentoring youth back in Atlanta? You guys should do something like that here at the shop."

The idea was exciting and certainly in line with the history of the shop. Jim had definitely been much more than a mentor, not only to Elijah but to Percey and Earnest as well. When he gave them jobs what he really gave them was a safe place to discover who they were. Earnest liked the idea of giving that same sense of worth and purpose to others.

Ma Eloise entered the office before anyone could reply to Molly's suggestion. She apologized for interrupting, but no one saw it that way. Everyone greeted her and they cleared a place for her to sit. Sharing an office basically meant twice as much paperwork in the same amount of space. Several chairs were now acting as shelves. Earnest Jay shifted the catalogues and files to the floor. Molly looked at the clock on the computer then apologized as she rushed to hug everyone goodbye.

"But honey you just got here," Elijah whimpered sweetly.

She sympathetically made her way over to give him a second kiss goodbye. "No, technically, *you* just got here," she offered him one last kiss then turned to leave.

When she was gone Elijah leaned towards Ma Eloise confidentially.

"Did you bring it?" He asked, finishing the last of the rice in his mouth. Ma Eloise pulled a small box from her purse and handed it to Elijah. He wiped his hands on his pants and grabbed the box, opening it carefully.

"Were there any problems when you picked it up?" He inspected the contents of the box to keep his nerves in check.

Earnest was out of his seat at the first sight of the ring.

"None at all. The clerk said they rushed to get it resized so it will be ready for your big dinner."

"I knew it," Earnest bellowed, "you liar."

Elijah laughed to himself without taking his eyes off of the ring. Truthfully, Elijah had been thinking about proposing since they'd gotten back together. The time apart had made him realize how much he truly loved Molly, and since Elsa's bed rest he had seen how strong they were as a team. He wanted to marry Molly, but seeing the ring made everything so real and he started to feel a knot in his stomach. Things were going so well that it was beginning to feel unfamiliar. Where was that other shoe or the storm clouds looming overhead? When and how was all of this bliss going to end?

He must have been thinking too long, because when he looked up Ma Eloise was standing behind him.

She put her hand on his shoulder and assured him, "You deserve to be happy baby."

"And so does she," Earnest continued. "Now if you'll excuse me," he walked toward the door intently, "I have a pool to start."

Elijah and Eloise laughed and he stood to embrace her.

"What part of strict bed rest is not registering with you woman?" Molly yelled playfully. Elsa Rae had gotten it into her head that she wanted to prepare an apology dinner for Bix to make up for how awful she'd been lately. Romance was in the air with Elijah's dinner plans only a day away and Elsa Rae was capitalizing on Molly's excitement.

"First off, you're carrying a human inside your body, you're allowed to be a little awful," Molly said to Elsa as they folded up the last of the baby clothes her in-laws had mailed. Lots of greens and yellows since no one knew the sex of the baby.

"Second, I know you're wired from all of the baby hype, but that is precisely why you should be resting." Molly made her point and glared at Elsa to make sure it really got through.

"Please, I promise I'll let you do everything," Elsa pleaded.

"Gee, thanks," Molly chuffed.

"No, you know what I mean. I'll do all of the work that I can from the couch and I'll order the food from Lilly's." She closed her hands in prayer then pouted to seal the deal.

"Tell the truth, is this about Bix or how bored you are?"

"Seventy/thirty," Elsa said dropping the charade for a moment to come clean.

Molly shook her head in pity. "Fine," she relented, "but one foot off of that couch and all bets are off."

"Deal," Elsa sang.

Molly spent the rest of the day cleaning and handing things to Elsa, but true to her word Elsa did all of her work from the couch. She called Lilly's and placed the order, picked out the dishes from their wedding china (although Molly was the one on a chair attempting to retrieve it), ironed the tablecloth, and arranged the flowers Molly picked from the garden. All that was left to do was set the table.

"Darn it, I forgot ice cream!" Elsa shouted as she folded the second cloth napkin into a little fan. "Howard always eats his pie a la mode," Elsa whimpered.

Molly knew that Elsa wouldn't quit. "If I get this ice cream..." Molly began with her finger extended at her best friend.

"Not one foot off the couch, got it." Elsa finished.

Molly grabbed her purse, annoyed with this new whinier version of her bestie. She called out her approximate return time then let the door close a little too loudly behind her.

Molly hurried back to the house, but when she pulled into the driveway Elsa Rae was coming out of the front door. Molly was already prepared to give her an earful when Elsa's words stopped her.

"Time to go to the hospital." Elsa shifted her overnight bag from one hand to the other.

"But, you're not due for two more weeks," Molly's voice was full of panic.

Elsa dropped the bag and gripped her belly in pain nodding profusely. That was confirmation enough for Molly, she sprang into action. She lifted the bag from the ground and rushed Elsa to the car. Her pants were wet and Molly realized her water must have broken already. Now she was terrified. How long after the water breaking did the baby come? She searched her mind for baby delivery references, which was mostly limited to movies and TV shows. She was certain it was different in real life, she prayed it took much, much longer than a commercial break for a baby to come.

"I didn't call Howard yet," Elsa seemed to really need him now. Frazzled, Molly tossed Elsa's bag in the backseat next to the ice cream and took off down the now darkening drive. *One thing at a time* Molly thought to herself.

The sky was a beautiful indigo still glowing with the last signs of day, but under the cover of the trees, the road was cloaked in darkness. Calmer now that they were in motion Molly took one hand from the wheel and placed it on Elsa's belly.

With her eyes still on the road Molly reached into the backseat to feel around for her purse. She felt her way to the cell phone and placed it in her lap. She took a deep breath to steady herself.

"I can do this," she whispered to herself.

"You can try him now," she mustered all the composure she could to sound calm. She handed the phone to Elsa, but before she could dial the number there was a loud boom and the car was thrown sideways then forward before everything went black.

Molly's eyes opened slowly to find Elsa staring blankly out of the front windshield. There was a thin line of blood on her cheek and she was hugging her belly, one arm underneath it and the other on top of it.

"The baby isn't moving," Elsa kept saying. "He always moves."

Molly's head felt like there was a drum line inside. She knew she needed to get them to the hospital but she could barely focus. She looked around to find the phone. It was on the dashboard close to the windshield. She reached out to grab it when out of the corner of her eye she saw a sudden movement. There was a large buck at the edge of the road staring at her. Molly froze until the buck limped into the darkness of the woods.

Molly looked back at the phone in her hand, it was shaking. She dialed 911 then lifted the phone to her ear.

Her sentences were broken and the sound of the operator's voice only made the throbbing in her head worse.

"Please hurry, she's having a baby," her voice trailed off and her eyes closed again.

She woke up as the paramedics were lifting her out of the car. She was trying to ask about Elsa, but the words were like peanut butter in her mouth, thick and sticky. One of the paramedics understood her panic and assured Molly that her friend was fine.

"The bag... she needs her bag," was all Molly could get out before her eyes closed again.

The next time she woke up she was in a hospital bed with Ma Eloise at her side. She was knitting a baby blanket. There were purple flowers in a clear vase on the table behind her. Molly smiled at the sight of them, certain they were from Elijah.

When she saw Molly's eyes open Ma Eloise drew closer to the bed. She welcomed her back with a gentle caress on the forehead and a kiss on the cheek.

"Is everyone alright?" Molly asked quickly.

"Everyone's fine. Baby Caleb is resting in the nursery," Ma Eloise assured her.

"Aw, Caleb," Molly sighed, resting her head on the pillow behind her, "it's a boy."

"Eight pounds and two ounces."

"Geez," Molly said, "that explains the bed rest."

She shared a laugh with Ma Eloise.

"Where is everyone?" Molly asked.

Ma Eloise's face changed. It was just for a moment, then the calm smile returned. Molly suddenly realized how strange it had been to find only Ma Eloise in the room when she woke up. Was everyone with Elsa and the baby? She moved to get out of the bed, but Ma Eloise stopped her.

"Everybody is a little worked up right now baby. Why don't you just rest?"

Molly had this feeling that there was much more going on than she knew. She couldn't shake this need to see Elijah. Weak and sore she pushed the covers back and grabbed the pole with the IV to steady herself.

One look at her face and Ma Eloise knew Molly was not going to be coaxed back into bed. She decided instead to simply make sure Molly didn't stumble and fall. She wrapped the blanket she had been using herself around Molly's shoulders and they made their way into the hallway.

Ma Eloise showed her the way to Elsa's room. Elijah and Bix were standing outside talking. When Bix saw Molly he turned abruptly and stormed into Elsa's room. Molly could feel the ground underneath her cracking, like a frozen lake. She was beginning to feel that there would be no one left to help her if she fell in. Her hand slid down the IV pole from the sweat on her palm. Elijah's back had been to her but when Bix left he looked over his shoulder at her and took a deep breath before walking over to her.

He was cordial but he was standing too far from her and he wouldn't look at her. Her mouth felt dry and her chest tightened.

"Elijah," she said reaching out to take his hand, "what's going on?"

He looked down at her hand she could tell he didn't want it there, but he didn't move it, yet.

Crack.

"You should get some rest," he said finally looking up at her.

Molly didn't sense concern, the statement felt like a warning. Her heart raced and she wondered how much longer her legs would hold her up.

Elijah turned away and began to walk back to the room. Tears burned in Molly's eyes.

"Elijah!" she yelled.

He turned on his heels and marched towards her. She would have been afraid if she weren't so relieved, coming back meant he cared. He was angry and sad, but at least he still cared.

"I asked you to take care of one thing for me. Not just one thing, *the* one thing I care about in this entire miserable world, and she's laying in that bed unconscious. I never ask anyone for anything, but I asked you."

Crack… Crack…

"It was my fault. I let myself want something," he glared at her with a thousand curses in his eyes. "But it won't happen again."

Whoosh… She was under the frozen lake now and it was hardening above her. She was drowning in the hallway of that hospital and just as she predicted there was no one there to save her.

"Where is Molly?" It was the second thing Elsa wanted to know when she woke up in the hospital two days later. The first, of course, was about the baby.

The nurses headed out to bring her new son, Caleb. She and Bix had chosen to continue her mother's tradition of using a name from a favorite story in the Bible.

She was excited to share the moment with her superhero of a best friend. Only no one was giving her an answer and neither Bix nor Elijah could look her in the eyes.

Her excitement quickly turned to worry, "Where is Molly? Is she alright?"

Bix assured her that Molly was fine. Ma Eloise had taken her home the day after they were admitted. When Elsa pressed about why Elijah didn't take his girlfriend home instead of Ma Eloise, Elijah informed her that no formalities had been overlooked as Molly was not his girlfriend anymore.

His timing was impeccable, because the nurses walked in with baby Caleb just in time to save both he and Bix from Elsa's wrath.

After a couple of hours of cooing, Elijah was sure he was off the hook, but when Caleb fell asleep in Elsa's arms she laid him in the bassinet beside her and wasted no time revisiting the subject of Molly's absence.

Bix, uncharacteristically angry, vented his fury first. He started by admonishing Elsa. How could she ignore the doctor's orders about bed rest, and for ice cream? Elijah added his disapproval, but insisted that the true blame belonged to Molly who was supposed to be the one ensuring Rae stay put.

She let them vent and scold her like a child. She fumed silently and waited patiently while they explained that Molly was no longer welcome in their family.

Elsa mustered the little calm she had left, "What direction was the car facing when you found it on the road?"

Bix and Elijah looked at each other confused. *What did that have to do with anything?*

"Was it headed to the house or from the house?" She pressed before either could answer.

"How did my overnight bag get here Howard? Did you bring it?" She pointed to the bag in the corner. The outside was covered with ice cream and neither of them had even noticed it was there until now. Bix was starting to understand.

"I asked Molly to help me plan a dinner. For *you*," she pointed aggressively at Bix, "and she wouldn't let me lift a finger the entire day so *she* cleaned and set up while I made phone calls from the couch. By the time she got back from picking up the ice cream so you could have your pie a la mode," she turned to Elijah now, "I was already in labor."

Bix sank back onto the wall. He was beginning to feel sick.

"On our way to the hospital a buck rammed the car. Molly, with what I can only assume was a concussion, called 911 and told them where to find us."

There was only silence—thick, shameful silence that felt like a punishment.

"Elsa, we…" Bix tried.

"You know what the most upsetting part of all of this is? Not that Molly missed out on seeing Caleb, who she fought so hard to get here, not that she felt rushed to leave a hospital she was recuperating in, but that the people she counted on most were willing to believe the absolute worst of her when all she's ever shown them is her absolute best."

They were quiet again.

"I'd like you both to leave." She said in a dangerously low tone that neither had ever heard from her before.

"But Elsa," Elijah objected.

"Get out!" she yelled and the sound was so explosive that it roused Caleb from his sleep. The nurse came in a moment later. Bix looked over his shoulder as he and Elijah exited, but Elsa would not look up at him.

Several hours later Elijah and Bix found themselves at the table of the only sports bar in town with Earnest Jay as their third. Bix filled him in on all of the details while Elijah silently sulked into his beer. He realized now that he shouldn't be angry at Molly, she had done everything right, but somehow that only seemed to make him angrier. And there was nowhere to put it all. He felt like his whole being was full of something he desperately needed to get rid of, only he didn't know how.

He knew what *should* happen next—he should go and beg for Molly's forgiveness, he should tell her how wrong he was to assume the worst of her and how bad he felt for abandoning her back at the hospital. But those all felt like lies. He wasn't really sorry at all. He was somewhat remorseful about hurting Molly, but he meant what he said at the hospital. Why wasn't he allowed to be pissed about yet another near-tragedy in his life?

"Elijah," Earnest Jay roused him from his thoughts a moment later.

"Where were you just now?" Bix asked.

"Probably on Molly's front porch with a guitar," Earnest and Bix tried to laugh as Elijah looked away again, this time pretending to watch the game on the TV across the bar.

Bix stood from the table and drew his wallet from his pants pocket, Elijah motioned to tell him he could put it back and Bix thanked him. He wanted to see if he could beg his way back into his wife's hospital room before it got too late. Earnest agreed that it was getting late for him too. He'd volunteered to open and close the store so Elijah could take a few more days with Rae.

Elijah stayed behind. The thought of going home alone made him even more restless. When Darby Wilkes came to the table later to close out his tab he returned her flirtatious smile and it occurred to him that he did not have to.

They stumbled into his apartment in the middle of the night, kissing and peeling off clothes like they were on fire. They were both burning to get rid of something, or to get something. Elijah pressed her to his torso with his hands grasping at the arch of her naked back, and for a moment he thought about kissing Molly on her bed, his hand slowly curling around her waist as she kissed him with her eyes still closed halfway between sleep and awake, like he was the dream.

He pushed the thought of her away as Darby pushed him back onto the couch and stood above him so he could look at her. But all he could see was Molly laughing on the couch in her parents' basement, arm stretched across the back of the couch and her head resting on it. Darby leaned down to kiss him, but all he felt were Molly's lips brushing against his on her front porch after their first date.

He took Darby's arms and gently pushed her away as he sat up on the couch. He apologized then stood to put his clothes back on.

"You can take the bed," he said pointing back to the bedroom. She kissed him goodnight, but it wasn't fire she felt for him now. It was pity. How could she shame him? She was half naked in the carriage apartment of a man she barely knew. *How dare she pity me?* But deep inside he understood how worthy of that disappointment he really was. At least she knew what she wanted.

She turned back at the edge of the room, "I'm sorry about your sister's accident," she said sweetly then turned to continue down the hallway to the bedroom.

Outside, Molly spotted the half-naked Darby heading to Elijah's bedroom from her car in his driveway.

The next morning Molly was at her kitchen table drinking coffee when she heard a knock on her porch door. It was Bix, or Howard, she wasn't sure if you could keep calling someone a nickname if you weren't friends anymore. It seemed like one of those things you negotiate in a divorce settlement.

"I thought I'd try to catch you before you head out to work," he said. Molly gave the ok and he entered the house timidly. He was hiding something behind his back, but not very well.

"I'm out sick," she said staring into her coffee mug. He inquired about her early rising if she wasn't going in to work.

"Couldn't sleep," she shrugged still not looking up.

"I brought you this," he said revealing a bouquet of flowers and a gift bag. Her curiosity outweighed her suspicion so she took them both and opened the bag.

"I love this show," she said as she lifted a box set of her of her favorite superhero TV series out of the bag. Her excitement was too pure to be contained.

"You're fighting dirty," she said tossing him a sideways glance. "I respect that," she held out a fist for him to bump.

He laughed, but it sounded as much like relief as it did amusement.

Molly stood from the table and made her way towards the cabinets to get another mug. She lifted the coffee pitcher as an offer, Bix nodded in acceptance.

"So I take it you're still in the dog house with Elsa?" She said.

He lowered his head in mock defeat, before assuring her that his apology had much more to do with realizing how wrong he was for punishing her.

"I didn't even give you a chance to explain." He was stumbling through a very heartfelt apology when she put her hand on his.

"I get it," she said earnestly. "Your wife and child were in danger. You did what dads do, you were standing up for your family."

"Yes, but I should have given you the benefit of the doubt. Especially after all you've done for us," he said with a resolve that only someone as serious as Howard could manage.

"Maybe," Molly said smiling "but it would have been easier to do if someone else was leading the way."

His smile faded a bit. He knew what she meant and she was right. At the time he believed he was doing what Elsa couldn't, he was standing up for her. The action may have been wrong but his intent was pure, he wanted what was best for Elsa and Caleb. But Molly was alone with no one to defend her, no one to stand on her side and fight for her. He felt for the first time how broken that must have made her feel and he reached out to take her hand. Her eyes began to well up and she pulled her hand away and stood, pretending she needed to pour more coffee for herself. So Bix pretended not to see her wiping her eyes. It occurred to him that was what she had been doing before he showed up, she had been crying. He wondered how long, had she been crying all night? The thought was too upsetting, he changed the subject.

"Elsa and I were thinking we could all watch the show together. You haven't met Caleb yet."

"So, what you're saying is that my present is really a present for you?" They both laughed. "No really, I'd like that."

CHAPTER 15

Movie Night

Earnest Jay hadn't seen such sharp turns since ROTC in high school. Molly had just spotted him in the cereal aisle of the grocery store and she'd turned so fast to avoid him he could practically feel the wind from her escape on his face.

"Molly," he called as he chased her down in the ethnic foods aisle. "Will you slow down?"

"Wasn't sure we were allowed to talk, I figured it was against the rules or something," Molly said not looking back at him, when he finally caught up to her.

"You're mad."

"No," she barked picking up a bag of pinto beans that she knew she wouldn't buy. "Ok, yes. I know you and Elijah are friends. I just sort of thought that we were too."

"We are."

"Pretty sure friends visit friends in the hospital."

"And I did. Of course you were pretty out of it with the whole head injury thing but I was there with Aunt Eloise. I even sent you some flowers, didn't Elijah give them to you?"

Now it was beginning to make sense.

"No, but I got them."

"Hey, you ok?"

And something about the way he asked so quietly made her feel overwhelmed. Sad and angry she began to cry. Earnest Jay pulled her into his arms and held her there waving away nosy strangers passing by.

More composed, Molly laughed to herself and wiped her eyes. When she was finally done crying he wouldn't let go until she promised she was ok.

"I'm fine," she offered. "Elsa, Bix, and I are having a sort of movie night tomorrow, do you want to come?"

"Is there going to be more crying," he asked. Molly laughed out loud she was so tickled.

"I hope not," she wiped her eyes.

"Man, I was really looking forward to that," he said.

She laughed again as he hugged her goodbye.

Holding a baby for the first time is a miracle. It is the only time Molly could ever remember truly believing in the concept of love at first sight. Caleb was so small and beautiful. He needed so much that Molly wanted to give him everything. She couldn't imagine being Elsa, of loving him more than she already did. She thought her heart might explode and she was only the "auntie."

"He's so beautiful you guys."

"He's alright," Elsa joked.

Molly looked up at her and smiled.

"I missed you so much," Elsa said to Molly and both of their eyes began to well up.

"I missed you," Molly replied.

"And I missed you too," Earnest mocked before insisting they pause the love fest and watch people beat each other up instead.

Bix pressed play and everyone's eyes turned to the screen. Everyone's eyes except Molly's, she watched Caleb.

"I can take him if you want," Bix offered after noticing she was missing her favorite show.

"No, you cannot. We're making up for lost time." Molly said as she pulled Caleb closer to her heart. He seemed to be soaking up every moment.

"You have a party and nobody invites me?" It was Elijah's voice. Molly's heart sank and she froze. The rest of the room paused in awkward silence dividing their attention between Molly and Elijah. Molly sat still, wishing she could disappear. Bix asked Elijah for some help in the kitchen. When the men had gone Elsa turned to her and gently moved her hair from her forehead behind her ear. Molly began to tremble. She knew Elsa hadn't meant to remind her of her brother, but she had. She felt sick.

"You ok?"

"Mm-hmm," Molly lied. The hmm had gone an octave too high. This time it was Earnest who stirred. He wasn't sure when it happened, but by now he considered Molly a sister as much as he did Elsa. Up until now he had been a neutral party trying to remove himself from the situation by focusing on the television. But when he looked up at Molly's face all of the color was gone, she looked sick and he suddenly had the urge to punch Elijah in the chest.

Elijah left shortly after "helping Bix in the kitchen" but the effects of his presence lingered and Molly spent the rest of the night pretending to watch the show. Elsa pretended not to watch her worrying. As soon as the credits rolled on the third episode they all decided to call it a night. Molly couldn't leave fast enough and the moment she got in her car she was so relieved to be free of pretense that she forgot how sad and angry she was. The drive home was comfortably silent. She pulled into her driveway and slowly made her way up onto the porch.

"Hey," an all too familiar voice called out and she almost fell back down the stairs.

Her hand was on her heart. She looked at the porch swing to find Elijah sitting there. She rolled her eyes and continued up the stairs. *How dare he sit there?* She opened the door and trudged inside, she was too tired to have this conversation. Ever. There was not enough energy on the planet to express how truly disappointed and disgusted she was with him.

"Molly," he called, but she didn't answer. She took off her shoes and headed straight for the bedroom.

He waited for a moment, frozen in disbelief, then followed her into the bedroom.

"Get out Elijah," she said it quietly, but he could hear the anger brewing behind her voice.

There were suitcases on the bed and boxes on the floor.

"I'd like to talk to you."

"Why would I care at all what you want," she spat the words out like poison.

"Because you love me," he declared as if it were an undisputable fact.

Before she could stop herself she rushed at him and punched him in the chin. It was a solid punch, but he could tell she'd hurt her hand too. He grabbed her wrist, flinging her into the living room and onto the couch.

"Are you selling this house?"

"Why do you care?"

He started towards her so fast he half expected her to slink back in fear, but she didn't.

"I built this house with my own two hands, I slaved over it and now you want to just give it away?"

She stood and moved an inch from his face. "Now you know how it feels," she growled through clenched teeth. He grabbed her and kissed her, hard and mean and with no regret or restraint. She pulled away and slapped him with her ailing hand. She bowed over it in pain, almost certain it was broken. But when Elijah reached for her she pulled away from him. He didn't like the way it felt. It seemed too permanent, like this space between them was forever. He reached again and she moved to the other side of the room.

"I'm not Darby, Elijah, you can't just decide you want me and have me."

He flinched, how could she know that? Why did she know that?

"Molly—"

The House We Built

"Liar," she yelled. It didn't matter what he had to say, as far she was concerned everything about him was a lie.

He tried to start again but she wouldn't let him.

"When did I ever lie to you?" he yelled to top her so she could hear him.

"Every time you said you loved me. News flash—this isn't love Elijah, hurting people, abandoning them when they need you most, showing up on their doorstep at midnight accusing them when you should be apologizing."

"I never lied to you! I did love you, I do love you. I want to marry you," he said.

"Liar," she said with a quiet coldness that gave Elijah chills. He reached in his pocket to take out the ring, but before he could she spoke again.

"Why would I trust you to make me a promise like forever when you broke the very first one you ever made to me?"

"I never broke—"

"You said you wouldn't leave!" She yelled, refusing to let herself cry in front of him.

"You sat in my parents' house looked me straight in the eye and promised you wouldn't leave me. A month later, *one* month later and you didn't just leave, you tried to make me believe it was my fault."

She was breaking him. Couldn't she see that he wasn't strong enough to see her like this? He needed to make things better. He moved closer, he wanted to hold her and make all of this go away. But he couldn't.

"It wasn't your fault," he said softly.

"I know that," she barked back. "And if you'd given me a chance that night in the hospital I could have told *you* that."

He buried his chin in his chest.

"You don't want to marry me, Elijah. You don't want to marry anybody." She had her second wind now. There were still tears, but this wasn't crying, this was purging.

"You're already married, to you." He looked up at her. She wasn't making any sense, either that or she was making perfect sense and he was too scared to tell the difference.

"Your losses, your tragedies, your hurt, your pain. There's no room for anybody else in there."

"So I should just forget every bad thing that ever happened to me? Is that it?" The old anger was rising in his chest again. "We can't all live in the enchanted forest like you do. Some of us have real problems, real life tragedy that doesn't ask permission to interrupt our storybook endings," he exploded at her.

"So because I don't wear my sad story around my neck like you do, I don't have one?" She started towards him.

"Elsa went through everything you went through and she would never hurt anyone like you hurt me," she was close enough to touch him now, but she wouldn't.

"Or Ms. Eloise, she lost her husband and her son and she still made room in her heart to love you and Elsa like you were her own."

There were tears in both of their eyes now.

"Or Jim, or your mother…"

He looked up at her quickly. Those names were too sharp, they cut too deep and she knew that, but there were tears on her cheeks and he couldn't hate her when she looked that way.

"Or me." Her voice was trembling now and he reached out to take her face in his hands, but she stepped back so he couldn't touch her.

She steadied her voice, "You have no idea what I've been through, no clue how hard or easy my life has been."

"Whose fault is that Molly," he asked quietly. "Whose fault is it if I don't know you?"

One rogue tear forced its way down her cheek, but it wasn't sadness she was feeling it was fury. She was so angry she was trembling. How dare he ask her to share more of herself when he hadn't even protected what she'd already given?

She walked to the front door and opened it for him to exit. As he moved toward it she moved away. He stood in the frame of the door knowing this was goodbye. There was nothing he could do to change it, so he lingered to make it last longer.

CHAPTER 16

Tempest

Elijah couldn't sleep. He tossed and turned and tried to read or watch TV but nothing helped. At a certain point in every effort he realized how completely he had destroyed his relationship with Molly. And this, unlike all the other losses in his life, was entirely self-inflicted. He had sought this pain out. He had courted it.

The next day he went in to work at the shop, but his focus was divided. When Earnest had to stop him from giving too much change for the third time in a row, he banished Elijah to the office so he could get his head together.

An hour later Earnest entered the office with two cokes and demanded to know the latest installment in the saga that was he and Molly. Elijah told him that the saga had undoubtedly come to an end. When Earnest insisted that he and Molly would find a way to work it out Elijah silenced his doubt with the details of what happened.

"What is wrong with you?" Earnest said.

Elijah laughed, but for once Earnest wasn't joking.

"I don't know," Elijah responded when he finally grasped how truly unfunny it all was.

Elsa busted through the office door, "What did you do?"

Earnest took this as his cue to exit.

"Molly called me this morning, barely coherent, to say goodbye, her brothers are here loading up her furniture right now," she finished, winded from fury. Elijah was off of his chair and headed for the door before he could stop himself.

"Where are you going," Elsa asked annoyed.

"I'm going to go talk to her," he stated plainly.

Elsa walked over to block the door. "You've done enough already," she said.

He stared at her then took a seat at his desk. Elsa was right. He hated how mad she still was with him, but she was right. She turned to leave, opened the door, then paused. She stood in the doorway for a long time deciding whether or not to leave. Finally, she turned back and perched on the edge of the desk in front of her brother.

"You know who I think you're really angry with? God." She said it without giving him a chance to answer.

"I think you're afraid that if He exists, He'll want something you can't give."

He sat quietly, he wasn't sure she was right, but he knew enough to know he wasn't going to get to speak again until she was done.

"The thing is Elijah, I think what God wants more than anything else is you."

The words made him think of being back on those stairs with Molly, *I don't care if you're broken as long as you let me see you.* Had God been waiting for him quietly all those years the way Molly had waited with him on those stairs? And if so, why did He continue to take from him? Why did meaningful relationships in his life end in tragedy and pain? Wondering to himself was not enough, so he asked Elsa.

"Elijah, you're so focused on what we lost, what about everything we've gained? Sure we lost mom but we had Ma Eloise. You lost Mr. Jim, but now you and Earnest are closer than ever, and if it wasn't for Jim leaving *him* the shop he would have had nothing to come back to after he left his firm," she reasoned with him.

"Our lives are more than just what happens to us. It's about how we use those things to affect the lives around us," she said. "If we're drops in a bucket there should be ripples. You understand?" She stood from the desk, rested her hand on his shoulder then left.

"Knock, knock," Earnest Jay announced himself before entering Molly's house. Her brothers were already hard at work packing up her books in the living room. Molly gave a quick informal introduction. They nodded quick hellos and returned to their work.

Earnest never realized how many books she had until they were all stacked in piles on her floor. The room looked empty without them. Molly looked up from her work in the kitchen and smiled. It was weak but sincere. Her right hand was bandaged, so she was doing most of the work with her left. He walked over and gave her a hug.

"What happened there," he asked lifting the hand that was wrapped.

"Packing accident," she answered shrugging.

Earnest wondered what kind of packing accident bruised the top of her hand instead of the bottom. He could see that her brown skin was now slightly blue and purple under the bandage.

"So the rumors are true then," they both knew it wasn't a question, but Molly drew her eyes away to avoid it anyway.

"Where do you need me," he asked realizing how little she wanted to talk. She smiled and handed him the water glass she was holding and some newspaper.

"We're trying to get as much stuff packed up as possible so the guys can get in front of the storm on the drive back," she said glancing back at her brothers.

"Another storm," Earnest repeated.

Molly smiled, but the memory of the last storm she'd weathered in this house made her smile fall.

"Relax, it's just a little lightning," Earnest Jay joked, trying to cheer her as he wrapped more glasses.

They worked but never spoke. Molly put on some music to distract from the sad silence and every now and then she looked up and smiled a thank you at Earnest and her brothers for allowing her the solace of her own thoughts.

"How is she," Elijah asked Earnest when he got back to the shop later that night.

By now the thunder was rumbling like an ominous warning. Exhausted as he was, Elijah knew he wouldn't sleep again. His apartment was starting to feel smaller and smaller, like a trap. He turned the latch and twisted the knob and the thick, humid air felt like freedom. He walked to the shop to lose himself in his work. When he got there, Earnest Jay was gathering up empty boxes to take back to Molly the next day.

"You should ask her yourself," Earnest said without looking up.

"I don't want to risk getting punched again," Elijah said taking a seat on one of the work counters and holding his chin.

Earnest Jay looked up at him, amused. "That's what happened to her hand."

"Is she hurt?"

Earnest registered the sincerity in his voice and made his way toward him.

"It's probably just a sprain. She could still move her fingers and everything." Earnest took a close look at Elijah's chin.

"She got you good, huh?" he goaded.

"Her right hook was pretty beautiful actually," they laughed at the thought of sweet Molly as a boxing champ.

"What do I do?" Elijah said once the laughter subsided.

Earnest took a deep breath, preparing himself to deliver bad news. "I don't think there is anything you can do. I mean her brothers just drove half of her stuff back home."

Elijah pushed himself up off of the counter and began to pace. "The thing is I never wanted anything the way I wanted her. Nothing. Not even this shop."

"You probably should have led with that last night," Earnest Jay said calmly.

"But I just couldn't, I mean I can't…" and he couldn't. He left the sentence and his voice trailed off.

"Elijah, you've always done this. As long as I have known you. You get something nice and you give it away. Toys, bikes, even girlfriends," Earnest Jay began and Elijah grew quiet as he started to remember the truth of what his friend was telling him.

"I used to think it was so selfless the way you always thought everyone deserved better, but now…" Earnest stopped himself and searched for the right words.

"Now what," Elijah asked impatiently.

"Now, I think you were just scared," the words hung in the air like thick smoke.

He knew the answer but he asked it anyway, "Of what,"

"I think you were so afraid of losing something that you gave it up before it could be taken away."

There it was, the truth. It finally had a shape and a name, Fear. And it was standing in the room naked and bold and staring back at him. He had punished himself for loving Molly for wanting to build a life with her, and he had done it in the cruelest of ways, he had punished her.

"Where are you going," Earnest asked when Elijah abruptly stopped his pacing and started heading for the door.

"I have to see her," he wasn't even talking to Earnest really. It was more a call to arms for himself.

"Right now?" Earnest asked. After all, the storm was imminent, and not just the weather. Molly had made it pretty clear that she didn't even want to talk about Elijah. Earnest couldn't imagine she'd want to talk *to* him.

"I have to," Elijah said, and he began to pace again. "Can I borrow your car?"

"One, you can't even think straight right now, and two it's about to be crazy out there," Earnest answered.

"Yes or no," Elijah asked agitated. Earnest took one look at him and knew he was going either way.

"I'll drive," Earnest said as he pulled his keys from his pocket and led the way to his car.

The road was dark save for their headlights and the lightning that seemed to be chasing them from the shop. Earnest was trying hard to focus on the road which gave Elijah the freedom to silently practice what he was going to say. It would have to be good, epic really. As far as failures his had been an Olympic champion. They were less than two miles from Molly's house when a streak of lightning pierced a clearing in some trees up ahead. Earnest stopped the car merely as a reflex, and he and Elijah both stepped one foot out of the car to get a look at what the lightning hit. This was one of those rare storms where there was no rain to calm the heat of the flashes and whatever had been hit was now sending small puffs of smoke up into the air.

"Elijah," Earnest started, his voice low but steady, "isn't that..." he hadn't finished the question, but Elijah's heartbeat was speeding.

"God, please no." It was under his breath not even a conscious thought, but it was the most honest prayer he'd ever prayed.

They ducked back into the car and Earnest sped off down the road as Elijah reached for his phone.

By the time they reached the house the whole thing was ablaze, even the stand alone garage was beginning to catch flames. Elijah wanted to do something, anything to stop it but it was too much. The fire was everywhere. Helplessly, he began to scream Molly's name, praying that at the very least she could tell him where she was. He walked to the back of the house where her bedroom window was and screamed even louder. He didn't even notice when Earnest Jay ran behind him, afraid he'd have to stop him from going in after her. He yelled her name but there was no response. It was the longest few minutes of his entire life, if felt like eternity, like damnation, as if this were his punishment for the way he'd treated the people he'd loved most. If Molly was gone then so was he. She was the last straw, he couldn't lose anything else.

Exhausted and hollow, he ran to the front of the house to find the fire trucks arriving. Elijah watched as they moved to unravel the hose, but they weren't moving fast enough. It was like they were all moving in slow motion. Why weren't they moving faster? Didn't they understand that there were *two* lives at stake? He moved towards the fire truck to help or to punch someone, but he wasn't sure which yet. He would know when he got there.

Earnest's voice stopped him. "She's here," he yelled above the crackle of the fire and the bustle of the firefighters.

Her car was pulling up the drive. She stopped and Elijah watched her get out, staring at her home. He made his way towards her but she was already starting for the house. She didn't seem to see anything beyond the flames engulfing the last of her dream. She ran past Elijah toward the house, "No!" she screamed and she wouldn't stop screaming. Elijah wrapped his arms around her waist from behind and pulled her close to him, but she was still reaching for the house, still screaming. He whispered softly that he was there, that they were safe, but it didn't seem to help. In fact, it seemed to make things worse, and then he realized *he* was why she was screaming. She didn't want to be comforted by him, she didn't want him to touch her. He had already burned everything they had and now this storm had come for the rest. He loosened his grip and left her to wail.

"It's all out," Elijah said as he walked over to the bench in Havoc's garden.

It was all that was left of the house, and Molly had been attempting to sleep on it for the last hour, refusing to leave until the fire was out. She was lying on the bench with her eyes open. The blanket that the firemen gave her was wrapped around her shoulders and Elijah and Earnest offered their jackets to make a pillow for her. She was still and quiet and barely blinking. There were tears still streaming from her eyes across her temple and onto her hand which was folded beneath her head. When Elijah reached the edge of the bench he touched her leg to rouse her she flinched slightly, not startled exactly, but on guard. He hated that, hated that he made her feel she needed to be guarded with him. Once he had made her feel safe, and now he was the enemy.

She sat up to make room for him on the bench. He lowered himself slowly beside her and they sat, quietly watching the sky grow a bright grey as the sun worked to force its way through the blanket of clouds covering it.

"You can go if you need to," she said, her voice still raw from mourning.

"I'd like to stay if it's ok with you," he said quickly.

There was no way he was leaving her alone, but he knew he was in no position to make demands. She nodded without speaking and they sat quietly watching the sky again. He caught a glimpse of her from the corner of his eye, she was crying again. Not loud or violently like the night before. Now she was barely moving, her face and eyes were forward but there were tears racing down her cheeks. They were on her neck before she reached to wipe them.

"What can I do," he asked quietly turning towards her. Her face was still as she shook her head.

"There's nothing left to do. It's all gone," she said so flatly that it scared Elijah.

She was empty, the way he had been last night when he thought he'd lost her. He understood her brokenness because he felt it. It wasn't just the house they'd lost; it was the last bit of who they had been together. Now there was nothing left. Or there seemed to be nothing left, but that couldn't be true could it? They were here, lingering near the smoke and ash together. He knew what he had to do.

It was risky, to give her what she needed would require another promise, and he had lost his credibility with her. But she had to know what he felt. He wanted her to feel the same hope. He slid closer to her and put his arm across the back of the bench behind her. He was careful not to touch her yet.

He leaned down and whispered into her ear, "Then we'll build it again."

Her lips quivered slightly then parted as she gasped for breath, she exhaled a soft cry. He wrapped her in his arms and held her there. And she let him.

EPILOGUE

"Guys, I cannot be late for my own opening," Elijah called from the bottom of the stairs. He was pacing slightly in the foyer in his new grey sweater, his hands in the pockets of his best pair of jeans. Earlier that day he had wondered out loud to Molly if a suit might be better.

"It might be more professional, but it wouldn't really be you," she said as she straightened out his clothes before kissing him and disappearing out of the room.

"Daddy, Mommy said James trew up again," Eleanor, their three-year old daughter, was still having trouble with "th" sounds. She hobbled down the stairs in her Sunday best. The sight of his daughter in the dress her Aunt Rae bought her was enough to melt his heart. Sunlight from the window was shining through her beautiful curly mane - she was perfect. He reached up and grabbed her from the stairs before tossing her into the air.

"He did, did he?" he said, pretending to be angry. She squealed with delight.

"Please no more accidents," Molly called from the top of the stairs holding their son James in one arm with the trendy changing bag her mother bought her dangling from the other. "I finally got everybody dressed."

Elijah reached up to grab the bag from her and gave James a quick kiss. When he leaned back he stood smiling to himself.

"What," she said, amused because he was.

"Nothing," he said grinning shamelessly. 6 years, 4 months, 2 weeks, and 11 days after the fire and Molly was still changing his life, still helping him become the best version of himself. He wasn't sure if there were words for that but he was excited to have the rest of his life to show her how happy she made him.

It had been a long road. After the fire Molly went back to Atlanta and stayed with her parents for a while. Ma Eloise and Earnest had arranged for their family to stop by the old house and help Molly by gathering up anything that looked like it could be salvaged. Everyone helped, everyone was allowed to help except Elijah. After the clean-up, Molly and her parents headed to Ma Eloise's for the infamous family dinner. Elijah made sure he just missed them. It was the first time Elijah missed dinner with everyone since college.

The moment on the bench had been beautiful, but there was much more damage done than a hug and a few words could fix. He knew it would take time and he graciously accepted his place outside the circle of trust until he could earn it again. They didn't speak for the first year after she left. The only news of her he had, he got from Elsa and Earnest, who had started working with her on the mentoring idea she'd proposed.

Elijah didn't push, he was patient. He even pretended to be happy for her when she started dating someone the following year. Elsa and Ma Eloise quickly made their feelings known and urged him to act before it was too late but it was Earnest and Bix who set him on a course that changed everything.

"You said you never wanted anything more than you wanted to be with her," Earnest said plainly over a round of drinks at the sports bar.

Elijah looked up from the table and smiled a "be careful" sort of smile at him.

"So prove it," Bix said matter-of-factly before looking up at him and smiling.

He needed to keep his promise. He knew what to do to win her, but he wanted to make sure there was someone left to win. He called her for coffee.

"Just coffee I promise. Earnest and I are in the city this week talking to some rec centers about the mentor program."

She knew what he was doing. He was buttering her up by mentioning the program. She knew it was a bad idea, especially since she was seeing someone now. She wished she could ignore the butterflies in her heart *and* stomach. But she couldn't.

"Ok," she said softly.

It was strange to see her after so much time had passed. She had always been beautiful, but somehow the recent tragedies had refined her features. She looked stronger, more poised. She'd cut her hair and it framed her face even more perfectly. She touched his arm and gave him a quick peck on the cheek when she arrived. It had only happened because she was flustered, if she'd remembered how upsetting this all was she would have pulled back and been distant. But she didn't want to remember, she was tired of remembering, it was making her a bitter person and she didn't like that version of herself.

They exchanged pleasantries and well-planned compliments. Neither wanted to go on and on about how good the other looked. It felt desperate, never mind that from either perspective it was the truth.

"So I heard a rumor that you're going to church with Bix and Rae now," she started when her coffee arrived at the table.

Elijah lowered his head and smiled.

"She finally wore you down, huh," Molly asked smiling.

He knew he had missed her smile, but now he felt it. Subconsciously he leaned in to be closer to her.

"I just had a few questions I needed answered."

Molly was trying not to show it but she felt the weight of him closer and she wasn't sure she disliked it as much as she should have.

"Did you get them," she asked, leaning back a little.

Elijah grinned to himself. He took the hint and sat back in his chair.

"Some of them."

"And the rest," she asked with curiosity blooming in her eyes.

"I think I got something better," he started. "I think I learned I was asking the wrong questions."

Molly pursed her lips in contemplation and Elijah laughed. He had missed how transparent she was, how she was never able to hide what she felt from him.

"I meant to apologize," she said taking off the scarf around her neck.
"For what?"
"Hitting you. That wasn't right, or fair."
"Molly that was like a year ago, and I'm pretty sure I deserved it."

Her lips tightened, she was trying to figure out how to say what came next.

"I don't think that's how love is supposed to work."

Elijah paused to look up at her, but she wouldn't look up at him.

"I think it's supposed to be about what we need, not what we deserve."

Suddenly Elijah remembered their second date. How she had changed his perspective with one sentence. And now she had done it again.

"That was the answer to one of my questions," she finished. She had been right that day—the view was the same, she was the same Molly, but now he was different. Unlike the man on that horse, this Elijah knew exactly what he wanted.

Two days later he was back in the office at the shop.

"Earnest, I think I have a project for your first group of mentees," he called out before he was even all the way through the door.

The plan had always been for a group of youth from the city to come out and learn about carpentry and construction during the summer. But what they would work on had never been decided. Molly had helped them with identifying the right teens for the task. They needed to be energetic but responsible. They didn't need to be angels, but they needed to be trustworthy enough to spend a summer away from their parents. Bix worked out an agreement with his Alma Mater to use the dorms for the summer, and Earnest quickly got to work on all the logistics and legalities that come along with working with children.

First, they got to work on clearing the land, and then Elijah worked with his new apprentices on the basics of building a frame. A year and a half and two groups of teenagers later, the house was built. Elijah had kept his promise, though Molly didn't know. She was helping from a distance. Partially because her expertise ended with programming and partially because she knew that being near Elijah meant being with him, and she didn't want that. Did she?

A lot had changed in the year and a half. Molly was drifting further and further from her life in Atlanta. She found herself much more passionate about working with Earnest and Elijah than she did about her job in the city and her relationship had cooled off. There had never been a real lasting connection between them. If she was honest, she knew it was because her heart was already engaged elsewhere. Not just Elijah, but most of her life was in that small town now—Elsa, Caleb, Bix, Earnest, and Ma Eloise—they were as much her family as her own mother, father, and brothers were. There were a few more family dinners after the first one and Ma Eloise and Molly's parents had become fast friends. Even her brothers had bonded with Earnest and Elijah over their similar interest in youth development.

"I can't just move there," she said to Elijah one night over the phone.

"Why not, you did it once before."

"Yeah, but I had a job and a house last time."

"You *have* a job here Molly, the only reason we're not paying you is because you won't let us. Earnest is applying for so many grants. He has at least three on his desk right now that could pay your salary for a year."

She couldn't let him hear it, but she was caving. The thought of being back there, back home, made her feel a peace she hadn't felt in quite a while.

"Ok, well Mr. Answer-for-Everything, where am I going to live?"

"You should come live with me," he said plainly, no joke or irony in his voice at all.

"I think that's the worse idea ever. Not to mention you live in a carriage apartment and your landlord is a racist who thinks I'll corrupt you," she laughed, but Elijah didn't.

"If you're serious about moving I think I have a place in mind," he said, plotting.

He had convinced Molly to come and see a property he'd been working on. He drove to Elsa's to pick her up and made her cover her eyes when they were a few miles away. Anyone else would have needed a blindfold, but Molly wouldn't cheat. She was the most honest person he knew, and she was beginning to trust him again.

He helped her out of the truck with her eyes still closed, stood her in front of the house, then moved his hand so she could see. She was silent. The cottage she once loved was nothing compared to this house. Two stories, a porch that ran the length of the house, and a brand new porch swing. The garden was even bigger, clearly Elsa's touch. The flowers were in bloom and Bix had added a bird bath. Molly smiled to herself when she thought of how everything began. She hadn't thought about Havoc in years.

She was silent, and Elijah took it as a good sign. He slipped his hand into his pocket and pulled out Ma Eloise's ring. She had given it to him when he told her his plans to propose in front of the new house.

"I know Jim would have loved Molly," Ma Eloise had said as she pressed her palms to his cheeks and kissed him on the forehead, "and I think it would make him proud to have her wear it."

When Molly finally turned around, already awestruck, Elijah was on one knee with a jewelry box in his outstretched hand. He opened his mouth to speak but she interrupted before he could begin.

"We should go," she said abruptly and started towards the car.

Elijah's heart sank but he knew this wouldn't be easy and he wasn't willing to give up that quickly. He cut her off before she could reach his truck. He pulled the door open, locked it from the inside, and shut it again.

"Don't," she said looking up at him with wide eyes.

It was a warning and a plea, but he didn't care. She pushed away and made her way to the other door, but he beat her to that one too.

"Don't what," he said as he locked the second door. "I was serious on the phone. I want you to live with me. In this house."

She pushed past him to check the window in the bed of the truck. It was a desperate move. She would barely fit through that window even if she could wedge it open.

"I want to make babies with you here and carry you to bed when you fall asleep reading on the couch."

She glared at him, annoyed, "Shut up Elijah."

He grinned. He knew her, she was angry but she wasn't done with him, not yet. Maybe she never would be, the way he never would. The thought of a life with him set her world on fire the same way it did his, and he wouldn't stop until he heard her admit it.

She made her way onto the porch and was trying to use the swing to block him, but she couldn't. He wasn't even near her yet, but she was right where he wanted her. "Tell me you don't want to be with me," he demanded, but he wasn't chasing her any more. There was no need, she couldn't escape him here. Not in their own home.

He slowly walked up the steps and she tried to move back, but there was nowhere to go.

"Tell me," he took her hand "you don't want to marry me," he pulled her close with his free arm around her waist.

There was no way out, she belonged here with him.

"Please don't," she managed as the tears began to flow.

"I won't, if you don't want me to," he said and her tears flowed faster.

"Molly, I am so sorry that I broke my promise to you, but I kept this one," he felt her begin to relax into his arms, she was still fighting him, but she was losing strength.

"I won't hurt you again," he said.

"Yes, you will," she said pushing him away.

She made her way around the porch swing and sat down. She wiped her eyes then looked up at him.

"We're going to hurt each other Elijah, we're human. We didn't end because you hurt me. You ended us when you wouldn't even try to fix it," she said weeping.

"That's all I've been doing for the last two years, trying," he tossed up his hands in frustration, before calming himself and walking over to kneel in front of her.

"You asked me if I got answers to my questions when I finally started talking to God," he was close to her face, but he wouldn't touch her. "I asked why I couldn't just fix things with you before. Why I couldn't just be honest about how afraid I was, and then out of nowhere I remembered this thing Mr. Jim used to say all the time. 'You can't fix anything with broken tools.'"

She loved him for that. Not for the house or the way he'd held her that morning after the fire or any of the thousands of moments they'd shared, but for this one. The one where he trusted her enough to show her who he was. This was the culmination of every other moment. And she loved him. He could see it on her face, so he opened the ring box and tried again.

"Molly Grasen, this house is yours no matter what your answer, but I don't want either of us to live in it without the other. Marry me," he pleaded.

She leaned in and whispered, "Ok."

He swept her up from the swing and held her for a long time before leaning back to look at her. He pressed his palm to her cheek and kissed her. It felt like forever since they'd kissed and no matter how much or how long it, didn't seem enough. It didn't seem like it would ever be enough.

She pulled away, then hugged him close and whispered, "Soon."

He laughed out loud. It didn't seem to be enough for her either.

Three months later they were married on that very porch. A year and a half later Eleanor was born. Molly insisted that she be named after Elijah's mother. And when their son was born almost two years later they agreed on Frederick James for her grandfather and James Hargro.

"I've learned that the most important tools are not the ones we use to build homes and furniture, but the ones we use to build each other."

Molly was radiating as she watched her husband speak from the lawn of his new business. With Willie's well under control, Molly had encouraged Elijah to pursue his own dream. He said "I always liked the idea of the last house I built being ours."

"When Jimmy made a place for me at Willie's all those years ago he didn't just help a boy find a livelihood, he helped me find myself."

Elsa made her way over to Molly, tears of pride already brimming over in her eyes. They hugged each other and watched Elijah speak the last of his dream into existence.

"And when my wife told me 'no' the first time," the crowd laughed, "she challenged me to be a better man than what I thought I could be."

He looked up to find her and when he did he held her gaze. A tear began, and Molly pulled Elsa closer.

"My sister, my mother, or rather, my mothers..." he said looking over at Ma Eloise who was holding Caleb and Eleanor on her lap, sitting in a section reserved just for her.

"...my friends," he tossed a glance at Bix and Earnest, "and my wife— these are the tools that help build me. So, yes we will build furniture here, but it will be my honor and privilege to help these young people build their lives, hopes, and dreams just as James Hargro helped me build mine. Ladies and Gentleman... the Hargro Studio for Custom Furniture Design."

He cut the ribbon then lifted his arm to point at the sign. He found his wife's eyes in the crowd. She glowed with a love so big he could feel it from the distance between them.